THE SUMMER MELT

A NOVELLA

EMILY MARCH

EMILY MARCH BOOKS

Published by Emily March Books

ISBNs 978-1-942002-62-8 (paperback) 978-1-942002-60-4 (ebook)

ONE

Something cold and wet landed on Dana Delaney's hands as she unlocked the back door of Scoops, her ice cream parlor in Eternity Springs, Colorado. Glancing above her, she grimaced. Snowflakes? Seriously? It was the seventeenth of May!

"Double Chocolate Toffee Crunch," she muttered, cursing in her own particular way. Nothing like springtime in the Rockies.

It might just send her to the poorhouse.

She stepped inside her shop, flipped on the lights, and stowed her purse and lunch tote in her office. Glancing at the wall clock, she read eleven fifty-one. She had nine minutes to complete the short list of daily tasks required before opening the store.

Not that she needed to worry about a rush of customers at noon. Oh, she would see her handful of daily customers, but unfortunately, this type of weather didn't bring in tourists and townspeople the way sunshine and warm weather did.

She needed sunshine and warm weather and tourists this summer. Lots of tourists. Lots and lots and lots of tourists.

Dana sighed heavily and went about her prep. She opened the front door at three minutes to noon and carried her broom outside to sweep off the sidewalk. An occasional snowflake continued to swirl in the gusty breeze. As she bent to sweep debris into her dustpan, a familiar voice called her name. Dana straightened and smiled to see her friend, Celeste Blessing, crossing Spruce Street from the Mocha Moose, holding a lidded paper cup in each hand.

Celeste was the owner of Angel's Rest Healing Center and Spa. Now a thriving resort, Angel's Rest had breathed new life into Eternity Springs when the small mountain town was in danger of dying. Celeste was exceedingly kind, beyond generous, and wise in ways that benefited all those who requested her counsel and advice. She had become the town's happiness ambassador. For Dana, Celeste filled the hole created by the passing of Dana's beloved mother and maternal grandmother.

Today, just like most days, Celeste sparkled. She wore a matching gold rain jacket and hat over skinny jeans. Her light blue eyes gleamed from beneath the wide-brimmed rain hat that sat jauntily atop her short, silver-gray hair. Her smile made the overcast day seem brighter. "Happy Tuesday, Dana," she said. "Do you have a few minutes for a cup of tea and a chat? I have a business proposition for you."

"I absolutely have time." Only a fool would be too busy to listen to a business proposition from Celeste Blessing. The woman had uncanny instincts.

Chimes jingled as Dana opened the door and gestured for her friend to proceed her into the shop. Celeste took a seat at one of the half dozen red-and-white-striped parlor sets that served as seating inside Scoops. After dumping the contents of her dustpan and stowing her broom, Dana joined her.

"I guess it's more a favor than a proposition," Celeste

began, scooting one of the paper cups across the table toward Dana. "It's about one of my summer employees. Have you met Rusk Buchanan?"

The name sounded vaguely familiar to Dana, but she couldn't place him. "I don't believe so."

"He's one of my study abroad students."

Then it clicked. The Colorado Rockies teemed with international students during the summer. "Oh, is he the guy that the teens in town are calling the 'Hot Scot'? I overheard the high school cheerleading team talking about him when they stopped in for ice cream last week. He's in one of the college programs but he's got the high school girls in a tizzy."

"That's him." Celeste sipped her tea, nodded, and sighed. "He's a sweetheart and an excellent worker. I hired him to lifeguard at the resort swimming pool, but it's not working out. Yesterday alone, we had three incidents of false cougar drownings."

Dana frowned. "False cougar drownings?"

"It's not just the high school girls who are in a tizzy. Females at least a decade older than Rusk who go into the pool—where the water is still quite chilly, mind you—and pretend to struggle to be rescued by a wet 'Hot Scot.'"

"Oh." Dana couldn't help but chuckle. "Oh, dear."

"Yes, oh dear. And that's only the older women. Once school lets out and the summer tourist season begins in earnest, my fear is that the swimming pool will be overrun. I don't want to have to close it to locals or institute a lottery system for daily entrance."

"That would be a shame." The Angel's Rest swimming pool was the only public pool in town, and it's where the majority of the children in Eternity Springs learned to swim.

"It's quite the conundrum. I would shift Rusk into a different job at the resort, except that would leave me short one lifeguard, and it's late in the season to be finding someone qualified."

"That's true," Dana agreed. Eternity Springs was a geographically isolated small town. Finding help was always a problem. Finding specialized help could be a nightmare.

"I have thought of one possible solution, but it involves you. So that's where the favor comes in."

Dana knew what Celeste was about to say, and her stomach sank. "You want to poach my assistant manager."

When Dana opened Scoops four years ago, Alissa Cooper had been sixteen and her first hire. She was intelligent, dependable, and trustworthy. She'd been a godsend for Dana.

She also was a certified lifeguard.

Celeste held up her hand, palm out. "Not poach. Hear me out, Dana. I know how much you count on Alissa. What I'm proposing is a trade. Rusk for Alissa. Of course, they'd both need to agree to the change, but based on comments Rusk has made, I feel confident he'd be on board. I didn't want to approach Alissa before I spoke to you. However, I suspect she'd like the job. You know how much she loves our pool. Last summer, she swam laps almost every morning before work."

It was true. Alissa would love to spend her summer outdoors. However, Dana identified one insurmountable problem. Grimacing, she said, "Oh, Celeste. I can't match Angel's Rest's pay scale."

Especially not this year, she thought, what with the bank loan she'd taken out last fall she had coming due at summer's end.

Dana wasn't getting wealthy with her ice cream parlor, but she made a decent living from it. And, she loved the life-style Eternity Springs offered. Ordinarily, she could withstand a year of bad weather. However, last fall she'd chosen to make a substantial donation to help with medical expenses for her oldest and dearest friend's seven-year-old son. Dana didn't regret incurring the debt for a minute, even if it did mean she had to sweat snowfall in May. Seven-year-old Logan Ellison had received his new kidney and was doing great.

"No worries, there. Angel's Rest will cover the difference. However, I don't think you've grasped the big picture, Dana. Think about it. Cougars eat ice cream, too."

"Oh. *Cougars.*" Dana sat back in her chair. The beginnings of a smile flickered on her mouth as she gazed through the shop's large picture frame window to the dreary, overcast afternoon. "Even when it's chilly, you think?"

Celeste's blue eyes twinkled over the cup she brought to her mouth for a sip of tea. "I have a hunch that Scoops will have a banner season with Rusk serving up dips of Royal Gorgeous Gumdrop."

"Okay then. I know better than to bet against one of your hunches. I'll talk to Alissa when she comes in. I'd also like to visit with your study abroad student."

"I anticipated that. I invited Rusk to stop in for an ice cream cone at twelve twenty."

Dana glanced at the clock on the wall and read twelve seventeen just as a tall, broad figure strode past the front window. "Celeste, you are a wonder."

The door's bells chimed, and a young man stepped inside. He nodded toward Celeste, then met Dana's gaze and smiled. *Whoa. Hot Scot, indeed.*

Rusk Buchanan was the very cliché of tall, dark and handsome, and his smile had enough wicked in it to tempt any female with a pulse. So, when his heavy-lidded green eyes focused on Dana, she instinctively wanted to preen—until he called her ma'am during the introductions.

"It put me in my place," Dana explained to her friend Amy Elkins when they met for a happy-hour drink after work.

"And reminded me that he's barely old enough to buy me a drink! He's an awfully cute fella though. If a Hollywood scout ever discovered him, he could easily be America's next heartthrob."

Rusk started work at Scoops the following day. By week's end and despite the lingering cold spell, Dana's daily sales had tripled. The young man quickly proved to be a collegiate champion flirt while working behind the safety barrier provided by the display case.

Warmer weather finally arrived and settled in with Memorial Day Weekend. Dana extended operating hours from nine to nine. Rusk worked the day shift, and Dana regularly arrived in the morning to find a line outside the door.

As the days ticked by, Dana worked long hours, stepping up production to keep up with demand, happy as a clam to be doing it. She had yet to begin dating again following the breakup of a longtime relationship last year, so putting in extra time at Scoops suited her perfectly. At the close of business each day, she made a silent toast to Celeste when she counted her receipts. If sales continued at this pace, she'd have her loan paid off by the Fourth of July.

Everything changed the second week of June when her phone rang at eight a.m. and Rusk Buchanan whispered, "Dana, I am unwell. I will not make my shift today."

"Oh, no! What's the matter?"

"I think the fairies came calling while I slept. They drove over me with a truck, banged my head with a hammer, and scraped my throat raw with a zester."

"Oh, Rusk. I'm so sorry. Do you have a fever?"

"No, but I do have a strange rash on my belly. I'm to see the doctor in a wee bit. I am sorry to leave you in the lurch."

"Don't worry about that." Though Dana couldn't help but have a flutter of concern. She'd had a horrible sore throat, fatigue, and a rash when she had mononucleosis in college. The illness put her down for the count for three whole weeks. "Follow the doctor's orders and concentrate on taking care of yourself. Get well soon, Rusk."

"I'll do my best. I will miss my daily dairy fix."

Dana decided she wasn't about to let her Highland Hottie do without. Arriving at Scoops early, she packed a half dozen pints of his favorite flavor and headed for his address, a garage apartment that Celeste provided at one of her rental properties. Dana climbed the wooden staircase to the apartment above the garage and knocked on the door. "Rusk? Special delivery. Pike's Peach is guaranteed to tickle your tastebuds and soothe your sore—"

The door swung open, and an invisible mule kicked the air right out of Dana's lungs. Because a stranger wearing nothing but gym shorts, sneakers, and sweat stood gazing at her with a curious look.

"Throat," Dana croaked. Actually, abs. A sculpted six-pack of them, covered by a light dusting of hair that arrowed downward to disappear into his shorts. And, *whoa,* she jerked her gaze upward, but it got stuck on shoulders. She'd always had a thing for broad shoulders on a man, and his spanned an area as wide as the front range of the Rockies.

He wasn't Rusk. He was a bigger, brawnier version of Rusk. An older version of Rusk.

Dana's new employee spoke of his family often. This must be his older brother, the former professional baseball player who had moved to Florida to live with their grandparents during high school. He now made his living as a highly successful sports agent. His name was Cal, she believed. Short for Calum.

Oh, wow. This Buchanan man was definitely old enough to buy her a drink.

Dana got a taste of the Hot Scot hormone rush that had tripled Scoops' sales so far this summer. Her heartbeat fluttered like a hummingbird's wings.

And that was before the slow, sexy smile softened his chiseled jawline, and his dark green eyes gave her an appreciative once over. Her mouth went dry.

Then he spoke. "May I help you?"

Hearing a faint echo of Rusk's Scottish burr emerge from Cal Buchanan's mouth spiked the temperature of the heat flushing through her. She feared her Pike's Peach might just melt all over the landing.

Wordlessly, she held up the basket.

His gaze focused on the ice cream pints in the basket she carried. Those gorgeous green eyes lit with pleasure, and Even Hotter Scot said, "Ah. You must be Dana Delicious."

TWO

CALUM BUCHANAN WAS A HAPPY MAN.

He'd awakened to a brilliant dawn and birdsong, and had gone for a long run on the trail around Hummingbird Lake. He'd begun a workout on the weight bench in his slob of a little brother's living room when a knock sounded on the door. Now a beautiful woman bearing gifts described to him as nectar from the dessert gods stood before him.

What a great little town Rusk had stumbled onto.

She cleared her throat. "*Delaney.* I'm Dana Delaney."

Dana Delaney had thick, auburn hair and big brown eyes. She wore an off-white, gauzy peasant top with laces at the scooped neck that begged to be tugged and hip hugging jeans. Long legs. The perfect amount of curves in all the perfect places. *Hmm. Think I'll stick with Delicious,* he thought. "Cal Buchanan. I'm Rusk's brother. I've come to visit for a couple of weeks." Taking a step back, he opened the door wider. "Rusk has told me about his job at your ice cream shop. Come on in."

"Oh, well, thanks, but I...um...better not. I need to open

Scoops in a few minutes. But I wanted to drop this off for Rusk first. Is he feeling any better?"

"Feeling better?" Cal glanced over his shoulder toward his brother's closed bedroom door. "He's feeling bad? I haven't seen him yet today. I got up early and went out for a run."

Delicious Dana explained about his brother's sick call. "Something cold and thick feels good on a sore throat, and Rusk does love his ice cream. Our peach is his favorite, so I brought some over."

"That's nice of you. Thanks. I'll see that my brother gets it." Some of it, anyway. No way was he passing along all six of the pints he spied in her basket.

"Great." Just as she started to hand over the basket, a raspy sounding Rusk called out, "Dana? Is that you?"

"Yes," she replied. "I brought you some of my special throat medicine."

"Please be telling me it begins with Pike's and ends with Peach?"

Her grin brightened the already sunny day. "That it does."

"Ah, ye wee sweet angel of mercy, will you bring it to me?"

Dana's concerned gaze met Cal's. "He sounds pitiful."

"He does." Of course, it could be an act. Maybe it was a ploy to lure his boss into his bedroom. Rusk had been bending Cal's ear about Dana Delaney for weeks now. Ordinarily, his brother wasn't the type to crush on an older woman, and Cal pegged Dana as being in her early thirties, but like the saying goes, there's a first time for everything.

From the bedroom came a thready, "Cup or cone?"

Dana smiled. "Pints. Plural."

"That's it. You have to marry me, Boss."

Cal snorted and met the visitor's gaze. "He's obviously

not *that* sick. Why don't you take him his ice cream? I'll grab a spoon from the kitchen."

"No need. I come prepared." She pulled a plastic spoon wrapped along with a napkin in cellophane from her basket.

He smiled down at her. "I should have known you would. His room is this way."

He turned to lead her through the maze of a mess that was his brother's living room when a sudden wind gust sent a loose shutter banging against the house, distracting both Cal and Dana. With her attention on the window, she failed to safely maneuver one of Rusk's junk piles. Cal saw her foot catch the center of a ten-pound hand weight.

It all happened in an instant. Dana squeaked, stumbled, and teetered. Cal turned and reached for her, hoping to prevent her from falling. The basket tipped, pints spilled.

Suddenly, he had a warm woman in his arms, and a cold carton of ice cream smashed against his naked chest.

Cal sucked in his breath. He smelled ripe peaches and something else from her shampoo. Roses, he decided. Despite the chill spreading against his chest, he didn't immediately let her go. Voice pitched low, he asked, "You okay?"

"Wow. Yes. Just peachy."

He smirked, and she continued. "How embarrassing. I think I tripped on something."

"A hand weight. It was lying beneath a t-shirt. My brother is the king of clutter. He hasn't yet outgrown the living-like-a-college-frat-boy stage of life."

"Well, he *is* still in college," she said, a bit of babble in her voice. "Is he in a fraternity? He's never said. Do they have fraternities at the University of Edinburgh?"

"I think so, but I went to school here in the States. Rusk didn't pledge a fraternity." And Cal really should let her go.

But, instead, he wanted to rub his chest against her and smear that peachy ice cream all over them both.

He let her go. The pint slipped to the floor as they both took a step backward. Cal imagined bending down to lick the ice cream off the swell of her breasts.

He wasn't a pig, however, so instead, he tore his gaze away from Dana as she plucked her shirt away from her skin. Then, glancing down at his own torso, he wiped up a creamy streak and then sucked it off his thumb.

"Excellent. Though I'm more a caramel man myself."

She was watching his mouth.

"Do you make caramel ice cream?"

She nodded. "Garden of the Gooey is a chocolate, caramel, and peanut mix."

"I like the name."

"It's derived from Garden of the Gods. Our flavor names are all Colorado-based."

"Well, Garden of the Gooey is right in my wheelhouse. I'll have to try it while I'm in town."

Rusk's thready call from his bedroom interrupted the moment. "What happened?"

"You left your dumbbell on the floor, dumbbell," Cal replied as he led Dana to Rusk.

For the next few minutes, he watched Dana Delaney fuss over his brother like a mother hen. Rusk did look pitiful, and Cal was glad he'd made a doctor's appointment. It was hard to have quality family time when one of them was on the disabled list.

"I need to run," Dana said, giving Rusk's blanket a pat. "Let me know what Dr. Rose tells you."

"I will. Sorry for the...." Rusk made a waving gesture toward Dana's shirt.

"Don't worry about it." Dana added, turning toward Cal, "Sorry to leave you with the cleanup."

"It's nothing. Won't take more than a minute, and I was headed to the shower anyway."

Her smile fluttered. "Nice to have met you, Cal."

"My pleasure." *Seriously.*

"Welcome to Eternity Springs."

"Thanks. I think I'm going like it here. I'll stop by your shop soon."

"I'll, um, look forward to it."

After he shut the door behind her, Cal put the undamaged pints of ice cream in the freezer then took a shower. Then, clean and dressed, he checked on his little brother and found Rusk lying flat with the half-consumed pint of ice cream sitting on the floor beside him. "You look awful."

He smiled crookedly but didn't open his eyes. "I feel awful."

"Sorry about that, brother. I'll bet if you get some good drugs, you'll be better in a flash."

"Hope so. Hate leaving Dana in the lurch. She borrowed money to help a friend's child get a kidney transplant, and she's counting on Hot Scot sales to pay off her loan. Great boss. Great person."

"Hot Scot?"

"I told you about the older ladies at the pool. They followed me to Scoops and brought their friends. Dana's having a terrific year with me serving up ice cream. I don't want her sales to drop off." He opened one eye and looked at Cal. "You could take my shift today."

"I could what?"

"Go in and work for me today. No, make that today and tomorrow. We'll see who has the best sales numbers. Compare your Wednesday shift this week with my

Wednesday shift last week. I'll bet you Thanksgiving dinner dishwashing duty that you can't top my numbers."

It was waving a red flag in front of super-competitive Cal.

He didn't have to think about his response. He didn't mind spending two days of this two-week trip to Eternity Springs with delectable Dana Delicious. "You're on."

That's how he found himself striding toward Scoops an hour later, wearing jeans, a solid green sports shirt that matched the color of his eyes, and his brother's name tag. He'd covered "Rusk" with masking tape and written "Calum" with a black marker.

This was war.

THREE

After leaving Rusk's place, Dana rushed home to wash and change clothes. She decided against trying to find someone to take his shift. For today, she'd put her production on hold and cover the counter herself. She fully expected that business would slow down once word got around town that the Hot Scot was M.I.A. today. She'd probably have a steady stream of shoppers throughout the day, but the teenage contingent of customers would likely disappear. Thankfully, she no longer worried about paying off her loan due to her banner June.

She was five minutes late opening the doors and had seven customers right off the bat.

By nine-fifteen, weary of answering constant queries about her absent employee, Dana was ready to put her phone on silence. She posted a notice on the door announcing that Rusk had taken the day off for personal reasons.

To Dana's surprise, customer traffic increased rather than slowed over the next hour. She was rethinking her decision not to send out an S.O.S. for help. Then, bent over the display case to scoop up a junior-sized cone of Denver Nougat for one of the young Callahan twins, she heard the doorbells jingle the arrival of another customer. Busy with her task, she didn't see who had walked into Scoops.

She did notice the seventeen-year-old head cheerleader at Eternity Springs High School widen her eyes and elbow a fellow cheerleader in the ribs.

Even as Dana digested that, the sound of Scotland drifted over her as soft as heather. "Looks like you need to put me to work, Boss."

She jerked her head around. "Cal?"

"I decided to sub for my brother if you'll have me. So, I'm all yours today and tomorrow. Want me to serve ice cream or work the register?"

"Wait a minute. You are going to work? Here? For me?"

"That's the idea."

"But…but…"

A cheerleader piped up. "You are Rusk's brother? Seriously? Oh, this is awesome! I'd like a single dip of Lover's Leap-o-Licious Lemon Custard, please. In a cup. What's your name? I can't read the tag."

"I'm Calum." He reached toward the box of disposable foodservice gloves, winked at the girl, and laid on the Scot. "Would ye mind helpin' me out with a wee bit of direction until I find me way around the ice cream case? Which tub is Lover's Leap-o-Licious?"

The girl sighed dreamily and pointed toward the carton. Calum met Dana's gaze with his brow arched in question. She was no fool. "I'll work the register."

And so began one of the most hectic days at Scoops that Dana could remember. Rusk was a collegiate champion flirt; Cal proved to be a pro. He was playful and sincere, friendly, but not too friendly, quick with compliments, and endearingly sweet with the children who came in for a treat. Combined with his physical sex appeal, Calum Buchanan hit it out of the ballpark as his brother's temporary replacement.

Dana and Cal both welcomed the text from Rusk that arrived around lunchtime during a lull in customers. He'd tested positive for strep throat and received a script for an antibiotic that should knock the illness out fast. Dr. Rose Cicero expected that he'd be able to return to work the day after tomorrow.

"Perfect," Cal said. "I'll win my bet and then get to work on the business that brought me to town."

"Bet? What bet?" Dana asked. And, she wondered, what business?

He told her about the challenge, and Dana couldn't help but laugh. "That sounds like Rusk. He tries to make a contest out of everything."

"He comes by it naturally. Buchanans are a competitive bunch."

"Your brother mentioned that you played professional baseball. You played for Kansas City?"

"And Atlanta and Boston. Played third base."

"And you won the Series."

"The team won."

Dana could tell from the automatic nature of his reply that he repeated the sentiment often. The humility only made him more appealing.

"Rusk says you have—and I quote—a verra large and bonnie ring to show for it. I'm curious. Do you wear it or keep it for special occasions?"

"I wear it for business purposes more than anything. The bling impresses." He paused, then narrowed those gorgeous green eyes and focused a considering stare upon her. "Maybe I should wear it here tomorrow. If we spread the news around town tonight, we'll get a bunch of guys in here wanting a look at it. You had three females for every male coming through that door today. Could be a big boost in sales."

"Whoa. You are competitive, aren't you?"

A sparkle entered his eyes, and his grin went a shade wicked. "Oh, lass. I always play to win."

The door opened, and a new wave of ice cream seekers flowed into the parlor. For the rest of the afternoon, the business didn't let up. Dana and Cal had no more time for personal talk, but he managed to include her in almost every conversation he had. While serving double-dip cones to a family of five making their first visit to Colorado, he asked Dana to suggest local activities to do and sites to see. Cal also brought her into the conversation whenever he complimented a young woman on her hair or eyes or clothing and thus made his light flirtation acceptable and appropriate. Once he discerned that he was dealing with a local, he made sure to include a question or two about Dana during his friendly chatter. By late in the afternoon, Dana was feeling a little bit unsettled. It felt like he'd learned everything but her current weight and bra size.

Of course, a man of his experience surely determined those particular details with a single once-over.

He'd ferreted out tidbits about Dana's love life, including scuttlebutt about her breakup with the vice-president of the local bank last summer. He'd also been told that Jonathan had decamped for a branch facility in South Fork. Having everyone knowing one's business was one of the crosses one had to bear when living in a small town.

In Cal's defense, he'd balanced his nosiness by returning the favor. He was totally open about the fact that he wasn't married, engaged, in a relationship, or even casually dating anyone currently.

Speaking to members of the Eternity Springs Ladies

Tennis League, he asked, "There's no reason I can't invite Dana out to dinner tonight, is there?"

"None whatsoever," said Lil Callahan.

"Absolutely no reason you can't," Lori Timberlake agreed.

"The Yellow Kitchen is the best restaurant in town," Jenna Murphy informed him. "Unfortunately, I doubt they have an available reservation for tonight. They stay booked weeks in advance this time of year."

Hannah McBride leaned forward and murmured. "You didn't hear this from me, but Murphy's Pub will have live music on the patio tonight. Somebody special."

Dana forgot her embarrassment at that. "Special as in family?"

"It could be that someone has some new songs he wants to try out somewhere other than the Last Chance Saloon."

"Oh. I'm going to Murphy's tonight." Then, because Dana wanted to take back some of the power here, she turned to Cal and asked, "Would you like to go to Murphy's Pub with me tonight? Their burgers are fantastic."

"Sounds great. It's a date."

Was it? A date? An official date and not just a hang-out? Dana wanted to clarify the question, but not in front of her avidly interested friends. "Good."

"What time shall I pick you up?"

Okay, that did sound like an actual, official date.

Hannah inserted, "He's planning to start playing around eight."

Dana met Cal's gaze. It was like falling into a green mountain forest. "Murphy's doesn't take reservations, so if we want to get a good table, we should arrive no later than six-thirty." Then, with a grin, she added, "That would give you plenty of time to work the room regarding your ring bait before the show starts."

"Ring bait?" Lori asked. "That sounds interesting."

Without shifting his gaze away from Dana, Cal ignored the interruption and suggested, "How about I pick you up at six? That'll give you and me time to talk before the schmoozing starts."

As a rule, she didn't leave Scoops until six, but she could cut out early once the evening shift was settled in. "Perfect."

The tennis league members exited Scoops holding ice cream cones, wagging their brows, and winking at Dana.

Dana didn't know whether to blush or chortle with glee. She had a date with Even Hotter Scot. How about that?

Later, she wasted a full ten minutes debating what to wear. She eventually settled on jeans, a simple V-necked cotton sweater, and her favorite necklace. She'd recently purchased the lovely topaz and silver pendant from Silver and Sparkles, the new jewelry store in town. Dressed up but not overdressed, she decided to put the finishing touches on her makeup. She stared at her reflection in her bathroom mirror and said, "Relax. It's a casual dinner surrounded by friends. Nothing to be nervous about."

When a knock sounded on her door at precisely six o'clock, she fumbled the lipstick she was adding to her small handbag. It rolled beneath her sofa. "Butter pecan crunch," she grumbled as she went down on her hands and knees to retrieve it.

It had rolled beyond her immediate reach. Lowering her shoulders, she extended her arm farther. Finally, her fingertips brushed the metal case. Gripping it, she withdrew her arm, rose, and then groaned with dismay. White dog hair clung to her brown sweater. Her terrier mix, Sunny, was a shedder, and obviously, the robot vacuum was not doing the trick.

Dana quickly tossed the lipstick in her bag. She hurriedly brushed her sweater with both hands and moved to check her reflection in the decorative mirror hanging the wall. Just how much of Sunshine's coat still clung to her boobs?

The question disappeared in a poof when she saw that she had an audience. Cal Buchanan was watching her through the sidelights.

"Pistachio Toffee Cream," she muttered beneath her breath. Heat flushed her cheeks as she dropped her arms back to her sides. Why hadn't she let the stupid lipstick be? How embarrassing was this?

His gaze slowly lifted from her breasts to meet her eyes. He smiled and waved. Dana groaned. Well, nothing to do now but soldier on and laugh at herself. Pasting a smile on her face, she answered the door. "Hello, Cal."

"Hi. You look great, Dana."

"Not too furry?"

His gaze swept over her, and he flashed a wicked grin. "Maybe in a spot or two. You have no idea how difficult it is to refrain from offering to help. But this is our first date, and I'm a gentleman."

Warmth washed through Dana once again. At this rate, she would soon wish that she'd worn a sleeveless shirt.

"So, dog or cat?"

"Dog. A terrier mix. She's a cute little thing, but she's messy. Her name is Sunshine. I'd introduce you, but she's spending the week up the mountain at a friend's summer camp. They serve troubled children, and Sunny has proven to be a great comfort-giver for the little ones."

"That's a generous thing to do. I'm a dog lover myself. Unfortunately, I travel too much to own one, but I'm hoping to change that soon." He gazed around her entry hall with interest. "I love your place. Old houses are something else that interests me."

"Really? You strike me as more of a contemporary guy."

"Wait until you know me better. You'll see otherwise. Tell me how you came to be living in a Victorian home in the middle of nowhere, Colorado? Are you an Eternity Springs native?"

"No, I grew up in Wichita, Kansas. I inherited the house from my grandparents, who purchased it in the 1980s from descendants of the original owner. It was built in 1898."

"Wow. So it's a *very* old house."

"Yes. My own special money pit. Upkeep got to be too much for my grandparents, and they let things slide the last few years. It desperately needs a new roof, and I dream of bathroom renovations in my sleep. But I do love it. Would you like a tour?"

"Absolutely. But, maybe when I bring you home? The clock is ticking, and we don't want to miss out on that good table at the pub."

Now, there was a slick way to get invited inside at the end of a date. However, Dana couldn't find it in herself to protest. "Sure. Let me get my purse."

He drove a Porsche 911, but Dana hesitated as he led her toward the automobile. "As much as I'd like a ride in your sportscar, it's only a two-block walk to the pub. Parking is always tricky to come by around Murphy's."

"Works for me. It's a fantastic night." At the end of her drive, he gestured to the south, "This way?"

"Yes." Dana waved to her next-door neighbor, who was up on a ladder painting shutters as they walked past. Next, she returned the greeting of another neighbor out on a bike ride with her two grade-school-aged children.

Cal and Dana walked in comfortable silence to the end of

the block. At the corner, she motioned to the left, and after they made the turn, Cal asked, "So, how did we do today sales-wise? Better than last Tuesday?"

"I had a feeling you'd ask that question. Worrying you'll lose your bet?"

"Not hardly. Besides, today is only a warm-up. Our bet covers tomorrow's sales. So knowing today's traffic will help me judge how hard to hustle tomorrow."

"I don't keep hourly records. Just daily sales."

"Did we beat last week?"

She pursed her lips to stifle a grin. "By twenty-seven dollars."

He made a pumping motion with his fist. "It's in the bag. Especially after I spread around my...what did you call it? Ring bait?"

She snickered, and he grinned at her.

"Something tells me that tonight is gonna be quite entertaining."

"Lass, at risk of sounding boastful, I don't believe I've ever been called a boring date."

That, she easily believed.

It proved true, too. At Murphy's, following a private wink toward Dana, he managed to subtly spread the word that he'd played third base for the Royals when they won the Series. Soon, he'd attracted a group of fans asking a wide variety of questions. However, no one asked about his Series ring.

More than once, Dana was tempted to introduce the subject, but she'd decided to refrain from taking sides in the contest, so she bit her tongue. Finally, Murphy's owner, Shannon Garrett, shooed the crowd away when she served the dinner they'd ordered—a burger for Cal and a Cobb salad for Dana. Halfway through his burger, Cal bemoaned. "I can't believe that no one has asked me about my ring. Usually, it's one of the first subjects people bring up. But, instead, I get questions about box scores and television announcers."

"The evening is young," Dana replied. "Patience, grasshopper. So, earlier today, you mentioned that business brought you to town. Are you here to scout Daniel Racine?"

"Daniel Racine?"

"Well, shoot. I guess not if you don't recognize Daniel's name." Dana knew from Rusk that Cal had translated his success as a player into a high-flying career as an elite sports agent. He represented superstars rather than rookies, so she wasn't surprised that he hadn't heard of the budding local star. "Daniel just graduated from high school. He's Coach Romano's star forward on the basketball team."

"Lucca Romano. He coached in the college ranks, didn't he?"

"Yes. Coach R took the Landry University Bobcats deep in the NCAA tourney. Sweet Sixteen, I believe."

"You know basketball."

"I do." She stabbed a slice of avocado with her fork. "I follow most sports, and I'm a big supporter of our local teams. Coach R thinks Daniel will make it to the pros."

"I'll put him on my radar. Thanks for the tip."

"So, back to my question? You're in town for business?"

"Yes." He hesitated before adding, "It's a bit of a top-secret mission."

"Now, that's intriguing."

"Sorry that I can't be more forthcoming."

"Not a problem at all. I totally understand. Look, I don't discuss my ice cream recipes with anyone."

A teasing light entered Cal's eyes. "Well, that's disappointing. I was hoping to charm Sinner's Prayer Strawberry out of you."

"Not happening."

He studied her, sipped his beer, then leaned forward. "That sounds perilously close to a challenge."

His voice's deep timber sent a shiver running up Dana's spine. "Perilously?"

"For you. I play to win. Always."

Rusty at flirtation, Dana searched for an appropriate response. Unable to come up with anything witty, she settled for a simple, "Hmm."

The light in his eyes positively wicked, Cal opened his mouth for another volley. However, before he managed a word, Celeste glided up to their table and lobbed a softball for him to hit. "Calum Buchanan, I'm Celeste Blessing, owner of Angel's Rest Resort. Welcome to Eternity Springs. I understand you earned a World Series ring. I hope we get a chance to see you wear it while you're in town."

"Bingo," Cal murmured for Dana's ears only. Louder, he said, "I do own a World Series ring. It's a whole lot of bling, so I don't wear it as a rule. Although, I have promised Dana that I'll wear it tomorrow during my shift at Scoops. I'm subbing for my brother from nine to five."

"Excellent. I'll be sure to stop by and get a gander at it. Now, about poor Rusk. I've heard he is under the weather. Please give him my best wishes for a speedy recovery."

"I'll do that. Thank you."

The exchange was just what Cal had needed to get the ring bait rolling. Soon he'd fielded enough queries about his career, the Series win, and his bling that Dana felt confident of brisk business tomorrow at Scoops.

"Poor Rusk," she observed during a break in the stream of people stopping by their table to say hello.

"What do you mean, 'Poor Rusk'?" Cal scoffed.

"You're putting your thumb on the scale. Or, I guess I should say your ring finger. It gives you an unfair advantage."

"She has a point," observed one of the three men seated at the table next to Cal and Dana. Tucker McBride and his family were regular visitors to Eternity Springs from their home in the Texas Hill Country. He sat with his cousin Boone and tonight's performer, Jackson McBride, another cousin of Tucker's. All three men had obviously been eavesdropping on Dana and Cal's conversation—and felt comfortable enough to comment on it. Such was the way of small towns.

Cal grinned at the observation, then shrugged. "Like I said, I play to win."

Boone McBride nodded and spoke in a sage tone. "All is fair in love and ice cream."

"I second that," said Jackson McBride. "Especially Dana's ice cream. Caroline, the kids, and I just arrived in town yesterday, so I haven't made it into Scoops yet on this trip. Do you have your Granite Mountain Crackle Crunch this season?

"I do!"

"Excellent. That gives me one more reason to visit you tomorrow." Then, glancing at Cal, he added, "I want to get a look at that ring."

"Well, I'd like to see one of your Grammys. My brother tells me Boone is storing one of them at his home."

"I won it in a bet," Boone said. "Horseshoes."

"I'll get it back next time we play," Jackson declared.

After that and with table space at a premium, Cal invited the McBrides to join him and Dana. Their date morphed into more of a group event. Dana didn't mind. In fact, she was secretly a little star-struck, seated between a famous and talented musician and former professional baseball player.

If only her twenty-year-old self could see her now. Or, Jonathan. What she wouldn't give to have her ex walk into the bar and see her now, seated at a table with four attractive and attentive men. Jackson, Boone, and Tucker were happily married men whose words and actions remained utterly proper. But they listened to her when she spoke. They respected her opinions. They genuinely liked her!

And Cal watched her with warmth in his gaze. He touched her hand when he spoke to her and casually rested his hand on her shoulder when he rose to shake hands with people to whom she introduced him. His casual touches and meaningful glances were balms to Dana's soul. She was over Jonathan. Nevertheless, her ex's disdain-filled treatment during the breakup had bruised her ego and wounded her self-confidence.

Being out with Calum Buchanan and exchanging friendly small talk with the Cousins McBride healed a wounded place inside her that she'd failed to recognize existed before now.

Murphy's erupted into cheers, applause, and whistles when Jackson McBride took the stage. He thanked the crowd and told a story about the first new song he was about to play. "Before I get started, my wife is home with our little ones tonight, but she asked me to tell you all how excited she is—how excited all of us are—to be back in Colorado. As much as we love our home in Redemption, Texas, nothing beats Eternity Springs in the summertime."

The crowd clapped and cheered.

"It's so nice to see old friends like Celeste and the Turners and the Romanos. It's also great to meet newcomers like Calum Buchanan, who's here tonight with Eternity Springs's own master of the summertime sweet, Dana Delaney. Calum is a former third baseman with the Royals. He'll be at Scoops tomorrow showing off his World Series ring while trying to win a bet with his brother, Rusk. Now, I haven't met Rusk yet, but word of him has certainly spread around Eternity Springs."

"He's the Hot Scot," a blonde coed called out.

"So I understand," Jackson drawled. A consummate entertainer, he worked the crowd by rolling his eyes in a way that conveyed his amusement at the nickname. "Apparently, the Hot Scot has overheated himself. He's home ill. The lovely Ms. Dana has expressed concern that the ring gives Cal, here, an unfair advantage in their friendly wager on who can bring more customers to the shop. So, to keep this competition fair, when you go into Scoops tomorrow to buy a frozen treat and spy Calum's World Series bling, be sure to declare whether you're Team Hot Scot or Team Bling."

"Team Bling!" Cal called out in feigned disgust. "You can do better than that, McBride."

"I'll do better," offered the coed.

From a table of women Dana's mother's age, a female voice called, "I'll do you."

"Now, now," Jackson chided. "This is a family pub. Speaking of family, let me give you a bit of background about the song I'm about to sing. My daughter Hailey…"

He smoothly transitioned into the musical part of his performance. The following two hours passed in a pleasant blend of music and merriment.

When the show was over, they said their goodbyes to the McBrides and other patrons of Murphy's. Cal clasped Dana's hand as he led her from the building. He didn't release it as they began the short walk back to her house.

They talked about the new songs Jackson had introduced tonight and marveled at his songwriting talent. Dana told him about her acquaintance with the McBride wives and shared some Eternity Springs insider info about others with whom they'd spoken at the pub. As they approached her house, Dana recalled the seed he'd planted earlier about seeing her home. Was she going to cooperate?

Yes, she thought she would. Up to a point. Her bedroom wasn't part of the tour.

"It doesn't speak well of me as a brother, but I have to say I'm delighted Rusk came down with a sore throat. Today has been an exceptionally nice day."

"It's been a lovely day," Dana agreed. "Thank you for inviting me to dinner, Cal. I had a great time."

"Me, too."

At her front porch steps, she glanced up at him and asked, "Would you like to come in for a nightcap?"

"Yes, I would. I'm dying for a tour of your house."

"Okay, great." After a moment's hesitation and inner debate, she added, "I'm happy to show you around downstairs."

He gave her a long look, then nodded. "Nothing wrong with red velvet ropes."

"Red velvet, hmm?"

"Fits the fantasy."

What fantasy? she wondered. For her own wellbeing, Dana thought it best not to ask aloud.

They climbed the front steps. Dana unlocked the door and flipped on the entry lights as she led him inside. "What would you like to drink? I make a mean old-fashioned."

"One of my favorites. That will be great."

She led him into the parlor, where she made the drinks. Then, she gave him the nickel tour. He seemed genuinely interested in the history of the house, the architecture, and the period pieces with which Dana had furnished her home. "I've found there is a delicate balance between history and comfort. My friend Celeste—you met her tonight—advised me to be selective when it comes to living with a dead relative's furniture. Once you take possession of them, they're all but impossible to give up. Whether you have a place for them or not."

"Isn't that what attics are for?"

"Not my attic."

"What's in your attic?"

"That, Mr. Buchanan, will have to remain a mystery."

Just then, the grandfather clock in her hallway sounded the hour. Cal finished his drink and handed her the glass. "I should probably say goodnight. We both have to work tomorrow. It's liable to be a crazy day, what with Jackson adding his two cents to the mix. Team Bling, indeed."

Dana laughed and set the crystal highball glasses on the parlor coffee table. "It's bound to be a record-breaking day."

"I'm looking forward to it." Cal reached out and caught her hand in his. Then he stepped closer and added, "And that has nothing to do with any bet."

Dana's heartbeat raced as he slowly, deliberately, slipped his hands around her waist and lowered his mouth to hers.

The first brush of his lips was as soft as a hummingbird's wings. Once. Twice. Three times before he fitted his mouth against hers.

Cal took his time with the kiss, exploring, savoring, stoking the embers of desire that had hummed inside of Dana since the moment he'd opened the door that morning. Had it been only this morning? As Dana melted against him, she felt as if she'd known him forever. She thought she could remain in his arms forever.

Forever ended a moment later when his mouth moved away.

"Ah, lass, that's as sweet a kiss as I've had in an age. Goodnight, Dana Delicious."

"Goodnight, Cal." *Captivating Calum,* she thought to herself. "I had a really nice time tonight. Thank you. I'll see you tomorrow."

"Tomorrow." He turned and headed for the door. Dana

followed him and watched as he descended the front porch steps. Then, just as she was about to close the door and float upstairs in a haze of happiness, he stopped and turned around. "Lass? About tomorrow."

"Yes?"

"What team will you be rooting for?"

She giggled. She hadn't giggled in years and years, but she giggled now. "I win either way, don't I? I think it's probably best that I don my zebra stripes and emulate Switzerland tomorrow."

"Neutral? You're gonna remain neutral? After that kiss?"

"Goodnight, Cal."

"Obviously, I'm gonna have to up my game next time."

Next time. Dana smiled as she shut the door and leaned back against it. "Team Bling?" she murmured. "Team Buzz is more like it. Or Team Blaze."

Though she planned to wear her black-and-white striped shirt tomorrow, she was definitely Team Even Hotter Scot, all the way.

FOUR

[Cal]

BY ELEVEN A.M., CAL KNEW HE'D HIT THE BET OUT OF THE ballpark. Business at Scoops more than doubled from the previous day, with the number of men walking through the front door skyrocketing. If anything, they were *too* busy, with customers having to wait in line longer than Dana preferred. Luckily, she'd had the foresight to have another employee on call, and Cal had a fellow dipper by noon.

While he thoroughly enjoyed himself, he was glad to have the help. The need to constantly show off his ring slowed his serving pace. Plus, he'd had to field about eleventy-billion phone calls from his clients. It didn't help anything that his butt was dragging today. He was weary to the bone.

He'd spent over three hours answering emails after his date last night. When he finally went to bed, he'd slept poorly, plagued by erotic dreams involving mint chocolate chip and his temporary boss.

Cal had enjoyed his date with Dana Delaney. She appealed to him more than any woman he'd dated in months. Years. Honestly, he couldn't recall ever being this attracted to a woman after spending only two days in her company and ending a date with a relatively chaste kiss.

Of course, most of the women he'd dated for the past eight or ten years wanted to hop immediately into the sack. That had suited him fine when he was younger, but casual sex no longer held much appeal. He was looking for something more. Someone who wanted more, too.

He liked that Dana made it clear she had no intention of showing him her bedroom last night. He'd enjoyed kissing her and leaving wanting more. Even if it had meant a restless sleep due to ice cream dreams.

He'd greeted Dana with a friendly kiss this morning upon his arrival at Scoops. But, unfortunately, from the moment she'd unlocked the door, he'd had no further opportunity to speak with her privately. So, he settled for a public flirtation spiced with a few private looks. That Dana flirted and gazed right back made the day all the more fun.

As the afternoon wore on, Cal acknowledged that he wasn't ready for the fun to end. His thoughts turned towards tomorrow when Rusk would return to Scoops and the balance of Cal's two-week trip to Eternity Springs. He would miss spending the day with Dana. He could stop by and visit, but a guy could only eat so much ice cream.

Three cones a day, maybe? If he cut them down to single dip rather than doubles. Or else…

A glimmer of an idea occurred as he dished up cones and small talk with the McBride family. He considered the idea for the rest of his shift, studying it from all sides. It might work. The more he thought about it, the more he believed it would work nicely. The old two birds and one stone trick.

All he needed to do was convince Dana to sign on to the plan.

He could make that happen. Selling ideas was a big part of his job, and Cal did excellent work.

He watched the clock. He knew he'd won the bet with his brother. The outcome of the team tally business remained the only uncertainty. Would it be Team Hot Scot or Team Bling? Dana was playing that one coy. Cal felt good about his chances, but it wasn't a slam dunk. Rusk had caught wind of Cal's ring plan and had rallied the troops from his sickbed. Even though the second competition was outside of the original bet, Cal was competitive enough that he wanted to win it, too.

Around mid-afternoon, Cal managed to glimpse the Team scorecard and discovered that the race was neck-and-neck. He turned up his charm level, and as the clock ticked toward five o'clock, he grew confident he'd emerge victorious in all competitive arenas.

When his shift ended and Dana retired to her office in the back to run a sales report, he made himself a double-dip cone and went to watch. "How are we doing? I know we beat yesterday's sales. I think there's a good chance I'm already ahead, even with four hours to go before close. So you'll be able to call it early. Rusk is so going to lose. He'll have to take my turn for dish duty at Thanksgiving."

She chastised him with a look. "You remind me of a four-year-old."

"Careful there. I'm liable to take that as a challenge, one that's much more interesting to think about than today's activity."

At her questioning look, he waggled his brows. "I'd be happy to devote some time and energy to proving my manhood to you, Dana Delicious."

She rolled her eyes and snickered. "You are such a guy."

"Thank you."

"That wasn't a compliment."

"Guess it's time to change the subject. You know, I thought Heartache Falls Fudge was my favorite all-time ice cream flavor, but this Grizzly Berry is beyond awesome."

"No need to sweet-talk me, Buchanan. Voting has ended. The contest is over. The votes are tallied."

He licked his ice cream and asked, "So who won?"

"Sales today were up thirty-four percent over last week."

"Scoreboard." He took a big bite of his ice cream.

"However…" Wickedness gleamed in her big brown eyes. "Team stats are more interesting."

Cal narrowed his gaze. Suspiciously, he asked, "In what way?"

"It's a tie."

"No."

She nodded. "It's true."

"I don't believe it. I kept track, myself. It might not be two-to-one in my favor, but it was a victory, a close victory."

"You didn't hear all the votes. You missed some during the rush around three p.m."

"Not that many."

"We had a substantial number arrive by text messages."

"What? Text messages! Who said people could vote by text?"

She shrugged. "I don't see anything wrong with it."

"I see lots wrong with it. Rusk probably reached out to everyone on his contact list and asked them to vote. It's voter fraud."

"This from the man who proudly used bribery to solicit sales?"

"You mean my ring? That wasn't bribery. It was advertising. So, did you vote?"

She gestured toward her shirt, crisp white cotton with black pinstripes.

"That's a copout."

"I owe you both."

"You don't owe me anything," he replied, replacing the teasing tone in his voice with sincerity. "It's been fun."

"It's been a lot of fun, and I appreciate it more than I can say."

"I'm glad I was able to help you." Cal noted the framed photograph of a boy on the credenza behind her desk and recalled Rusk's tale of Dana going into debt to help a sick boy. "Speaking of helping out, I understand that you organized a series of fund-raisers last year to help with the medical expenses of a child. I have clients who are always looking for a good cause to put their money toward. Does the need for donations still exist?"

"Absolutely. Logan got his transplant, but the family has enormous debt and ongoing expenses related to his care.

"If you'll give me the information, I'll see what I can do."

"That would be wonderful. Thank you." She gave him a brilliant smile and added, "You now have a lifetime, all-you-can-eat free ice cream pass at Scoops."

"I'll take it, and fair warning, you might just discover I'm visiting Eternity Springs more often than you'd planned. I'll try not to eat you out of house and parlor, though." He polished off the dip of Grizzly Berry and started on the Royal Gorgeous Gumdrop.

Dana tilted her head to one side and studied him. "I wouldn't have figured you as a Gumdrop guy."

"I'm down with trying new things. I'll admit I never would have put these two flavors together until about a dozen people ordered this combo. It's delicious." He paused a moment, then circled back. "So, you're going to vote for Team Bling, aren't you?"

"Wait a minute." She narrowed her eyes and studied him suspiciously. "Was this whole exchange just a bribe for my vote?"

"No! Of course not. It's totally legit. My clients need tax write-offs, and they appreciate those that actually mean something." He waited for a beat, then added, "But if it makes you see that I'm a wonderful guy worth voting for, well, then...." He took a bite of the sugar cone and shrugged.

She laughed, and a new voice entered the conversation.

"I knew I'd better drag myself from my sickbed to get down here and protect my interests," Rusk said. "He's trying to bribe you, isn't he? I knew Cal would try that. It's the way he operates. It's his job."

"Now that's just wrong," Cal corrected. "My job is to negotiate. Negotiating and bribery are two very different things."

"Whatever." Rusk dismissed his brother and gave Dana an eager smile. "So, what's the verdict? Did I come from behind and whip his arse?"

"Watch your language around the lady, and don't worry about my butt. How's your throat?"

"Good as new." Rusk waggled his brows at Dana. "What's the word, boss? Shall I cue up *We Are the Champions?*"

"I cannot believe how alike the two of you are," Dana observed. "I'm glad you're feeling better, Rusk."

"Thanks. Me, too. The bet?"

Dana chuckled. "Well, you shouldn't be surprised that sales are up over last week."

"By a substantial amount," Cal said, folding his arms. "Scoreboard."

Rusk waved that away. "He cheated with the Series ring business. I knew he'd outscore me there. What about the team competition?"

"I did not cheat." Cal fired back. "And allow me to point out that officially, there was no team competition."

"But—"

"You have Thanksgiving dish duty. End of story."

"But I won, didn't I?"

Cal met Dana's gaze, flashed a wink, then gave an exaggerated sigh. "Fine. You won."

Cal caught Dana's supportive grin, then continued, "Team Hot Scot. Selling it with sex. Next, you'll be auditioning for The Bachelor. Ma will be so proud."

"Just using my God-given talents. Ma *will* be proud." To Dana, Rusk explained, "She always liked me better."

"Uh-huh." Cal propped a hip on the corner of Dana's desk. "Rusk here grew up singing along to show tunes with our mother. She loves *Wicked.* Maybe that's why it's so important for Rusk to feel...." He sang the word. "Pop-u-lar."

"Funny as a crutch, Cal."

"Enough!" Dana raised her hands in surrender. "You two make me glad that I never had brothers."

At that, the Buchanan brothers shared a grin. "You done here?" Rusk asked Cal. "It's all-you-can-eat pizza night at The Yellow Kitchen. They have good salads, too, if you're still on that healthy eating kick of yours. But I need to eat. I'm starving."

The Yellow Kitchen was on Cal's list of places to check out for the project that had brought him to Eternity Springs. "Sounds good. Dana, would you care to join us?"

"The Yellow Kitchen pizza sounds divine, but I'd better skip it. I'm working tonight."

"You have to eat," Rusk said. "Come with us."

"I had a late lunch. I'll grab a sandwich at home when I'm done here. I need to catch up on production, or I'll be locking the door by the weekend."

Cal snapped his fingers. "I meant to tell you that I moved the last carton of Boulderscotch from the freezer to the display case about an hour ago."

"I noticed that."

"Would you like some help? I'm happy to drop back by after dinner and put in a couple of hours."

"Thanks. I appreciate the offer, but I'm set up as a one-person production line." Her eyes twinkled as she added, "Better to protect my secret recipes that way. Although…"

"Yes?"

"If you wanted to drop off a Timberlake Cobb salad, I wouldn't protest.

"We could get ice cream for dessert," Rusk said to Cal.

"Pizza and ice cream it is." Turning to leave, Cal paused in the doorway. "I'll be here with your salad when you close. As much as I love your ice cream, variety is the spice of life, so I'll bring dessert, too. Something…different. Hope you are hungry, lass. I have plans for you."

FIVE

"HOLY BUTTER CRUNCH TOFFEE," DANA MURMURED WHEN the Buchanan brothers exited the building. She fanned her face with an invoice from the nut supplier she used. The pair had ridden a tidal wave of testosterone into her tiny office, warming it as sure as her favorite space heater.

She laughed at herself. She'd enjoyed the day, and preened at being the focus of Cal's flirtation. It had done her wounded ego good. *Take that, Jonathan-the-Jerk.*

Dana went to work on an energy high, anticipating one more bite of the Buchanan feel-good apple today. She cranked up hard rock on the music system and accomplished twice as much as she usually did in three hours. Apparently Cal was good for increasing production in addition to stroking her ego.

He was sitting at one of the tables in Scoops when she came out to close. She wasn't surprised that he sat alone. After his closing shot, she'd been ninety-five percent certain he'd ditch his brother before returning.

Dana couldn't say she minded.

Once she'd flipped her Open sign to Closed, seen her

evening shift employees on their way, and locked the door behind them, she greeted him by observing, "That doesn't smell like a salad."

"I got you a salad, but I also brought you veal Parmesan. It's what I ordered, and my taste buds stood up and sang hallelujah. Figured I'd share the experience."

"Oh, I love their veal Parm. Thank you."

He opened the bag he'd had sitting on an empty chair and removed a plate and silverware. "A real plate?" Dana asked.

"This food is too good to eat out of a takeout carton. Besides, fair warning, it's a bribe. I have a favor to ask you."

"A favor? What kind of favor?"

He pulled a bottle of wine and two glasses from the bag, and then the box containing her meal, which he plated and set in front of her. "First, I need to ask you to keep what I am about to tell you to yourself. This is lawyers-and-non-disclosure-agreement big, but since this is Eternity Springs, I'll accept your word of honor, pinky promise, vow on your book of ice cream recipes—or whatever vow you hold supreme. Can I count on you for that?"

"Absolutely. I'm totally intrigued."

Except, when he casually added a votive candle and— be still her heart—a red rose in a bud vase, her attention was torn between what he was saying and what he was doing.

"I'm in town to scout locations for a high-profile event, and I want to hire you to be my local expert. I'll need an hour or maybe two of consultation, then a full day of your time for a test run." Then, he named a pay rate that caused her to all but fall out of her chair.

"What is this all about?"

"In the vault, right?"

She made a zipping motion over her lips.

"I need to plan a full day of over-the-top, Instagram-worthy romance that ends with a surprise marriage proposal."

Her stomach took a running jump off of Lover's Leap. *So, he's spent the past two days flirting with me, and he's about to get engaged? Boy, did I read him wrong.* Dana scoffed a laugh and asked, "You're getting married?"

"No. Not me. One of my clients."

"Oh. Well, good." Thank goodness she hadn't read Cal Buchanan that wrong. If he'd kissed her and flirted with her and brought her veal Parm while on the verge of getting engaged, he'd be a jerk on the level with Jonathan. "Who is it? What exactly are you asking me to do for this test run?"

Cal hesitated. "I think my client's identity is need-to-know information at this point. The test run will be a walk-through of the day we plan. I want to do it from soup to nuts. That's the only way to work out all of the kinks and make sure the day goes smoothly. The goal here is a perfect day."

"Huh." Dana took a sip of her wine. "So, this client of yours is too busy or too important or too full of himself to plan his own engagement?"

"Pretty much, yeah."

"Lucky woman he's marrying," she replied, her voice dripping sarcasm.

"All I'm going to say about that is they're a match made in heaven."

"Okay, then. Well." Dana hesitated. She took a bite of her veal to delay, then got distracted for a minute by the heavenly flavor explosions on her taste buds. "You need to plan a dinner at The Yellow Kitchen. Reserve the private room."

"I had the same idea about the restaurant. Didn't realize they have a private room. See? That's why I need you. So, what do you think?"

Dana realized that if she agreed to help him, the combined

efforts of the Buchanan brothers would have totally solved her financial problems. "Honestly, I'm both attracted to the idea and put off by it. If I was waiting on a diamond ring from a guy and he decided to outsource the event, I'd be ticked off."

"I'll keep that in mind if I ever decide to propose to you."

She choked on a bite of her side of spaghetti and had to lift her glass for a sip of wine to wash it down. "Why do you do that!"

"What?" Cal's eyes were laughing at her as he gazed over his glass of wine. "Shock you? Tease you? Flirt with you? Predict the future?"

"Blonde Brownie Swirl," she muttered.

"Okay, I have to ask you. I noticed this habit of yours yesterday and again today. Do you use ice cream flavors as cuss words?"

She shrugged. "I'm around young people a lot. I like to keep it G rated, and this way, I don't slip up."

"Ah, that makes sense."

He reached into the bag and pulled out another box. "Tiramisu," Dana said. "My favorite."

"That's what I was told when I asked."

"You asked? You have excellent instincts, Calum. You don't need my help planning a day of romance."

"Sure I do. I'm not usually so inventive. You inspire me."

There he goes again. Flirting must be instinctive to him. She'd better watch herself so that she didn't start believing he meant the flattering things he said.

"Tell me you'll help me, Dana. Please?"

"I'd be a fool to inspect this gift horse's mouth. Sure. So how do you want to begin?"

"Brainstorming ideas." He pulled two spoons from his magic bag. "You've had a long day, and I know you must be tired. Want to get together tomorrow for breakfast or lunch?"

"You brought me sugar that's not ice cream. We can start now. I always think better with a sugar buzz. So, a day of romance, hmm? What sort of budget do you have?"

"Unlimited."

"Seriously?"

"Seriously. My client isn't willing to expend brain cells, but he's happy to throw his money around. He has lots of it."

"Okay, then. This could be more fun than I realized. What about the date. Is it already determined?"

"Yes, July 17th."

"Ooh, that could be trouble. Any flexibility? It's the height of the tourist season, so many places are already booked, whether restaurants or inns or some of our more popular activities like river rafting."

"I'm afraid the day is set in concrete."

"Okay. We'll deal with it. I assume our mystery couple will need overnight accommodations? For how many nights?"

"Yes, two nights, minimum, but I'd prefer to book the week. They won't be arriving together, and my client is liable to be very late the night before. I'd like to have either two rooms in an inn or a house. Again, money is no object here."

"The obvious place is Angel's Rest," Dana explained. "But, I guarantee they are booked. That said, miracles tend to happen when you need them whenever Celeste Blessing is involved. You met her last night at Murphy's."

"The blue-eyed lady that sparkled."

"Yes. She's a good friend of mine. I can check with her and see what she can do if you'd like."

"Perfect." Cal nodded toward her empty dessert dish.

"Can I get you anything else? Want me to run across the street and bring back a cup of coffee?"

"No, thanks. I'm great. Dinner was wonderful. I'm hitting a wall, though. Think it must be the carbs. I probably should call it a night."

"All right." Cal rose and corked the bottle of wine. "I'll clean up here if you want to do whatever else you need to do before you leave."

A few minutes later, they exited the front door of Scoops and as Dana locked the door, he said, "I'll walk you home."

"That's not necessary." She returned the waves of a group of friends from church leaving the Mocha Moose.

"It's desirable. So are you. I'm hoping I'll score another goodnight kiss."

Since she wanted a goodnight kiss, too, Dana swallowed her protest.

The walk ordinarily took Dana eight minutes. Tonight, they strolled, and it lasted more than fifteen. They spoke about the day, some of the customers who'd wandered in the door. He asked her to tell him about being a business owner in Eternity Springs, the pros and the cons. "It sounds like a nice life."

"It is. I'm very happy here." Lonely since the breakup, she thought to herself, but that wasn't something she'd say to him.

As they approached her house, he said, "Tonight has been a great start on the proposal project, Dana. I can already tell you're going to save me dozens of headaches and hours of effort."

"I think it might be fun."

"When do you want to meet up tomorrow? Breakfast or lunch?"

"Breakfast. I'll be making ice cream all day tomorrow,

and when I do that, I usually don't break for lunch. Is seven-thirty too early for you?"

"Lass, I'm an early bird. That's the middle of my day."

Boards creaked beneath their feet as they climbed the front porch steps. Dana said, "In that case, want to come to my house for bacon and eggs?"

"Perfect. Both."

At the door, she fitted her key in the lock and twisted it, then turned to face Cal. "Thanks for dinner. Again."

"You are welcome. I enjoyed it very much. Again."

He kissed her, a long, luscious, delicious kiss.

When he lifted his head, Dana's hormones were shouting a*gain, again, again.*

"Sleep well, Dana D."

She waited until he was halfway down the porch steps to say, "You, too. Even Hotter Scot."

He missed a step but demonstrated his athleticism by quickly regaining his balance. Then, because Calum Buchanan wasn't one to allow someone else to have the last word, halfway down her front walk, he turned and called, "Dana? Any chance I could get both bacon and sausage for breakfast?"

"Well, sure."

"Good." The landscaping lights illuminated the wicked glint in his eyes and his mischievous grin. "The more time I spend with you, lass, the bigger my appetite gets."

SIX

BREAKFAST WITH DANA PRODUCED A PRICELESS COTTAGE reservation at Angel's Rest resort and a battle plan for the proposal project. Cal spent the next two days scouting locations, making plans, and extinguishing the fires that his job as a sports agent entailed. The longer he spent in Eternity Springs, the more he resented the intrusions.

He needed a vacation, an honest-to-goodness stretch of time gloriously unplugged.

He deliberately left his phone in Rusk's truck when his brother took him trout fishing early Friday morning on Angel Creek. With a flick of his wrist, he sent his line sailing and set the fly down gently. "I need more of this. I love to negotiate, but the hand-holding part of the business is wearing me down."

"So why do it?"

"It's the job."

"You don't need the job, do you? Can't you live off your investments?

"I've already retired once. It didn't work out."

"You weren't ready to quit baseball when your arm gave

out. Becoming an agent allowed you to remain involved in the business and still compete. You loved signing a star player as much as you loved winning a playoff game. But, from the sounds of it, that has changed."

"The players have changed. My peers are aging out, and the young guys come in with ridiculous expectations of what my job entails. You wouldn't believe the latest with Keefer Jennings."

"Let me guess. Mr. Golden Arm doesn't have time to sleep with his woman, so he wants you to do it for him."

Cal laughed. "It's almost that bad. He wants me to pick out her engagement ring."

"You are kidding. Tell him no!"

"I intended to, but I took his call while I was with Dana. She overheard enough of the conversation to get all excited. One of her friends is a custom jewelry designer in town who has diamonds that Dana thinks would be perfect. Dana thinks the sale would be great marketing for the shop."

"She's right."

"Yeah. And I haven't told Dana that the bride-to-be is an Instagram Influencer—with capital I's."

"So, are you going to take Dana ring shopping?"

"Today during lunch."

"You know how much fun it would be to text Ma with that little detail? You know how much she wants grand-children."

"Ha ha." The conversation was interrupted by a strike on his line. While Cal fought his fish, Rusk also had a strike. The brothers fished for another hour in companionable silence. It was only as they hiked back to Rusk's Jeep that he returned to the subject of Cal's job.

"You know, brother, Dad died when he was only fifty-three. Life is too short to do something you don't enjoy. I get that you don't want to retire and become a snowbird, but you should find something you enjoy that doesn't wear you down."

"Easy for you to say. Maybe I'll become a beach bum in the mountains. What's the name for that?"

"Rusk Buchanan."

"Better not let Ma hear you say that. She's counting on you getting that medical degree."

"I know. Ma has nothing to worry about. Despite my struggles last semester, I'm still on track. I'll be ready to shift into high gear after my summer here in the Rockies. Maybe that's what you should do, Cal. Find a way to bottle the mental health medicine that is Eternity Springs. Something about this little town just makes a man feel good, you know?"

"I'm beginning to, yeah."

Five hours later, after a morning filled with phone calls and frustration, Cal escorted Dana Delaney toward Silver and Sparkles Jewelers to buy an engagement ring. It was a surreal experience. He admitted as much to Dana.

"This will be my third time," she confided.

"You've been engaged three times!"

"No. Twice, a friend's boyfriend asked me to help him pick out the ring for my friend. It's a big decision. Some guys like to have a feminine viewpoint."

"Ah. Yeah. That makes sense." Still, Cal couldn't imagine buying a ring for any woman he didn't know well enough to be sure about what style of engagement ring she wanted.

Dana continued. "I've never been engaged, myself. I expected it to happen with one long-time relationship, but that ended last fall. How about you?"

"I've never come close," Cal said, wanting to know more about this ex. But before he managed to frame a subtly prying question, they reached the jewelers, and at the doorway, Dana paused.

"So, which way do we play this?" she asked. "Do we let my friend Amy believe you're buying a ring for your love, or do we tell her the truth?"

"I'm telling everyone I'm a celebrity's front man and leaving it at that. People are curious but respectful of the privacy requirement. That's another nice thing about Eternity Springs. I noticed that at Murphy's the other night. People left Jackson McBride pretty much alone."

"We have a lot of celebrities in town. They're accustomed to it."

Inside the shop, Dana introduced him to Amy Elkins. The jeweler was blond, petite, and pretty, and around his own mid-thirties, he'd guess. "I'm pleased to meet you, Calum. I'm happy to have the opportunity to earn your business."

Recently, Amy had obtained a collection of diamonds whose provenance traced back to the Kelsy Lake diamond mine, a now-defunct mine in northern Colorado near the Wyoming border. She'd branded them the Colorado Rocks. "Potential customers for these diamonds appreciate the home-grown aspect of the stones," she explained. "It's added value, and the price reflects it."

"Clever," Cal said with genuine admiration. Plus, a "Colorado Rock" was a perfect fit for his client since the likely future Hall-of-Fame pitcher was currently playing for the Colorado Rockies.

They discussed Cal's requirements for the "4 C's" of diamond buying—carat, clarity, color, and cut. Amy had three stones that met the qualifications. The choice between them was a toss-up. Cal asked the jeweler to make the decision. That left the setting design to select.

After studying Tami Styles' Instagram account, Cal

believed he had a good idea of the bride-to-be's preferences. "She's flamboyant with her costume jewelry, but her real stuff is classic and classy. That doesn't mean this ring shouldn't be eye-catching and, above all, Instagram worthy."

"I can do classic and classy. First, let me show you what I have already made up. Then, if nothing appeals to you, we can work on a sketch. You want a platinum band, I assume?"

Lifting his shoulders, Cal looked at Dana. She nodded. "Yes."

Amy disappeared into the back of her shop and returned a few minutes later with five different rings. "I think these all fit your requirements."

Cal scratched the back of his neck. "Nice. What do you think, Dana?"

"They're all gorgeous. I'd love any one of them."

Amy observed, "Usually, a woman finds a way to mention what she wants to her man."

"Maybe she has, but that doesn't mean this guy paid any attention to hints she made. I just don't know." Cal turned to Dana. "Which would you choose?"

She moved two of the settings to one side. "These two are my favorites. Go with one of these and the Colorado rock. Both you and the groom will be heroes."

"Hmm." Cal studied the settings. The one on the right had space for two smaller stones on either side of the large diamond. The ring on the left would surround the diamond with smaller stones. He gestured toward the right. "That one looks like something you'd wear."

"In a heartbeat."

"It's pure class." Cal picked up the setting on the left and handed it to the jeweler. "This one has a shade more flash. Let's go with it."

"Excellent choice," Amy said.

Next she discussed the size and cut of stones she'd add to the ring. Seeing Dana's enthusiastic nod of agreement, Cal made a decision. "That sounds good to me. Could we do it this way? Would you set the stones, and I'll send a photo to my client for his approval before we finalize the deal? I honestly don't think he cares enough to veto this choice, and one way or another, I'm confident he'll go for the big stone. We can try the other settings until we have something he'll approve. Add extra charge for your time to whatever we end up buying."

Amy lit up like one of her Colorado Rocks. "Fabulous. I'll have it ready this afternoon."

"Great." He gave her his phone number. "Would you text me when I can stop by to see it? I have a three o'clock appointment, but it shouldn't last long."

Dana bubbled with happiness on the walk back to Scoops. "Thank you, Cal. Even if your celebrity doesn't publicize Silver and Sparkles, this will be a great sale for Amy. She's good people."

"Oh, I suspect you can count on it getting publicity."

"Excellent. So if your client okays the ring, will you bring it by and show it to me?"

"I will."

She beamed. "This is so much fun. I'm really enjoying your proposal project, Calum Buchanan. Thank you for including me." Then she went up on her toes and kissed him. Right there in front of Celeste Blessing and smack dab in the middle of Eternity Springs. Cal had a spring in his step as he went about his business that afternoon.

When his client called, he was about to enter the jewelry store to pick up the engagement ring. "Hey, Cal," Keefer Jennings said. "Those pictures you sent of the rocks got me thinking. I have an idea for the proposal."

"Oh?" This was a surprise. It was the first time that the athlete had shown any interest in the plans.

"I follow your brother on TikTok, and he's done a couple videos from that ice cream shop where he works. I think we should make the proposal there. I want to freeze the ring in ice cream and give it to Tami in a cone."

Cal lowered his phone from his ear and looked at it in disbelief. The volume level was high, so he could hear the pitcher's voice when he continued. "My favorite flavor is Rocky Road. Does that place make Rocky Road?"

"Wait a minute. You want to give Tami an engagement ring in a dip of Rocky Road? Message there, you think?"

"It's my favorite flavor," KJ repeated.

"Shouldn't you choose her favorite flavor?"

"She likes whatever I like."

And there is a match made in heaven. "Look, KJ. The ring won't show its best when it's covered with sticky ice cream. Plus, it's not beyond the possibility that she might take a big bite and swallow the damned thing."

"She won't do that. She doesn't bite. She licks." He laughed and added, "The woman has a talented tongue, believe you me."

Cal sighed and closed his eyes. And, because the needle on his patience tank was sitting at empty, he spoke without tempering his words. "It's a dumb idea."

It was the absolute wrong thing to say. Cal might as well have Facetimed and waved a red flag in front of the ball player because KJ dug in deep. "No, it's not. It's what we're going to do."

"I advise you—"

"I'm not taking your advice."

Cal opened his mouth. The words to sever their relationship hovered on his tongue. He was tempted...so tempted.

But damn it, he was looking forward to the proposal dry run with Dana. He could always fire KJ afterward.

Plus, Cal was too good a businessman to act on emotion. "All right. I'll set it up."

"Good. Remember, I'm the one getting engaged here."

"Oh, I remember." *I'm just shocked that you do, too,* he thought to himself.

He turned the conversation to a sponsor proposal for KJ that he'd received by email earlier that morning. Upon ending the call a few minutes later, he opened the jewelry store's door and stepped inside.

Amy was busy with another customer, so he perused the jewelry cases while waiting. She designed some pretty things. They definitely had a style to them. A look.

A pair of emerald drops caught his attention. *So, Dana likes emeralds, does she?* Maybe he should get her a thank you gift.

A few minutes later, the other customer departed, and Amy smiled and said, "Calum, I'm so sorry to keep you waiting."

"No problem at all. I've enjoyed perusing your work. I really like your style."

"Thank you!" She beamed. "I have your ring ready. I'll bring it right out."

"Excellent."

He exited Silver and Sparkles twenty minutes later. Outside on the street, he thumbed open the black velvet box. Catching the sunshine, the ring sparkled like sunlight on the surface of Hummingbird Lake. He murmured, "Team Bling indeed."

Well, at least Dana and Scoops would benefit from the publicity. Though for her sake and for the success of the proposal project, he needed to make sure it would be positive publicity.

As an athlete and a successful businessman, Cal understood that proper preparation prevented poor performance. The ring presentation needed to be a part of the run-through, so he placed a call to Dana to facilitate this last-minute change. When she answered, he asked, "I believe you said you're working production today?"

"Yes."

"What flavors are you making?"

"Today it's Mountain Mango Tango and Vistas Vanilla Crunch."

Hmm. Neither one of those was chocolate. "Could I talk you into making a small batch of Rocky Mountain Road?"

"I made that yesterday. I have five three-gallon containers in the freezer."

He thought about it. Guess they could hand pack a particular gallon to use. Or, maybe a pint. But no, a brand new carton would present better. "Could you make a small batch for me?"

"I guess so. Why do you need it?"

"It'll be easier to show than tell. I need to be there. When do you think you can start it?"

Sounding mildly annoyed, she said, "It'll be at least an hour. Probably closer to an hour and a half."

"That'll work. I'll see you then. Thanks, Dana." He ended the call without allowing her to ask more questions. Then, with time to kill, he decided to drop by the Mocha Moose and try today's coffee special. A coffee snob from way back, Cal was impressed with the Mocha Moose's bean selection.

It proved to be a productive afternoon. Cal enjoyed a long conversation with the Mocha Moose's owner and learned a couple of new tricks to try next time he had time to indulge in one of his hobbies—coffee bean roasting. Cal strode into Scoops a few minutes before five, waved at Rusk, who was finishing his shift and made his way to Dana's production kitchen.

In the process of cracking eggs into a bowl, she glanced up and met his gaze. "Good timing. I'm just getting started on the Rocky Road, and I'm curious to learn why I needed to make it. But first, did you get the ring?"

At his nod, excitement lit her eyes. "Let me see! Let me see!"

He pulled the ring box from his pocket and tossed it to her. She opened it, squealed, and gushed about its beauty. Then, when the oohs and ahs finally faded, Cal dropped the proposal bomb on her.

Dana's eyes went round. "Seriously? He wants to do it here?"

"Yes."

"Wow. Okay. Well, good for me, but frankly, Scoops doesn't occupy a top ten spot on the list of romantic places."

"Then it'll be our job to improve its placement. It'll be worth your while, I suspect. I've decided I need to tell you who will be the stars of the show."

Her eyes gleamed, and she rubbed her hands together. "Secrets!"

"Swear to silence."

"I swear."

"The bride's name is Tami Styles. Tami with an I. She's an Instagram Influencer."

Dana whipped her phone from her pocket. A moment later, she asked, "@TamiStyles4U?"

"That's her."

"Whoa. This is awesome for Eternity Springs. She has about a gazillion followers."

"Yep. The groom is—"

"Keefer Jennings!" Dana whipped her head up from her perusal of Tami's social media to meet Cal's gaze. "She's dating the Rockies starting pitcher!"

"Yes."

"Oh, wow. That's celebrity with a capital C, and now your date makes more sense. This is happening during the All-Star break. But, isn't he playing?"

"Not this year. KJ is on the Disabled List."

"Oh, wow. Wow. Wow. Wow. This will be huge for the entire town, probably as good as when the cooking show filmed here years ago. I visited my grandparents that summer and Eternity Springs was wall-to-wall people. And you plan to film the proposal, right? Inside of Scoops?"

Cal told her about the pitcher's Rocky Road cone request. She steepled her hands in front of her mouth. "Oh, dear. I don't think that's a good idea."

"I know. I tried to talk KJ out of it, but his head is as hard as his ego is large."

"The bride could break a tooth. She could choke on it. Even if she finds it okay, the ring will look awful all covered in chocolate. Oh, Cal. This could be really bad."

"I know. That's why I want to video the presentation rehearsal. Maybe when KJ sees how horrible the ring looks all covered in cream compared to how it looks against black velvet, he'll change his mind. I also want to see how difficult it will be to clean the ring once she discovers it. It has to be Instagram ready, after all."

He offered to help, but she had a system, so he grabbed a dip of Gold Miner's Maple Walnut, sat on a counter stool, and visited with her while she prepared the flavor. They talked about their families and his work and her book club's reading choices for the rest of the year. Then she asked about the plans for tomorrow's dry run.

"I want it to be a surprise, just like the actual proposal will be. All the elements should be as close to the real proposal as possible so KJ can see what it will look like in reality, as opposed to whatever he's currently envisioning in his head."

"Who will be playing the bride?"

"Hmm—do you have any recommendations? I'd ask you to play that part the entire day, but you should really be rehearsing your own role in the proposal itself, since you'll be the one who hands over the ring."

"I'll think on it and let you know. For my part, what should I wear?"

"Another good catch, Dana." He considered the question. "If you could dress similar to what Tami will wear, that would be helpful. Try to match her style in a low key way so the photos look elegant."

"And what will she wear?"

"Based on her Instagram…for a weekend in the mountains…shoot. I don't know. Probably not outdoors gear, but something she could pick up at a boutique in Vail. Is there a shop like that here in Eternity Springs?"

"Yes. At Angel's Rest. But I'll figure something out."

"I have an account set up there. Go buy a new outfit and charge it to your room." For Cal's preparedness plan, Dana would be staying at Angel's Rest tonight because that's where the happy couple would begin their day. Unfortunately, the actual cottage hadn't been available, but Dana had a lovely room in the main building tonight.

"I don't need to do that."

"Do it. It's a business expense. The service you're

providing this project is invaluable. Get something you love and let KJ pay for it."

"I'm tempted. I haven't bought anything new all year." She glanced at the wall clock. "I'm pretty sure the store closes at seven. I won't have time to shop."

"What is left to do?"

"The ice cream will be ready for the ring in a few minutes. After that, it's mostly clean up."

"I can handle it for you. It's only fair since you'd be done already if I hadn't asked for the chocolate. I know where most everything goes."

Dana took a look around her workspace, then nodded. "There's not too much to do. Okay, Buchanan. Knock yourself out. Give the Rocky Road about ten more minutes to firm, then sink the ring. The consistency should be such that it will level out on its own, but if not, just use a spatula and smooth it."

"Aye Aye, Captain. Anything I need to do to help with closing?"

"No, my night crew will handle it."

"Excellent." He rose from his seat, walked to the sink, and washed his hands. Drying them with a red gingham towel, he said, "I planned to begin the day with a sunrise breakfast at Reflection Point, but KJ advised me that Tami isn't one to get up before dawn. However, she does love pampering, so you'll start the day with a spa appointment. I'll pick you up afterward at nine-thirty. Our first activity is brunch, so plan accordingly. Anything you need or want tonight or tomorrow before I arrive, just charge it to the room."

"How fun. I could get accustomed to this. I'm really looking forward to tomorrow. It'll be fun to live the high life for a day."

"I'm looking forward to it, too." Cal approached her, cupped her cheek in his palm, and stared into her eyes. "I want it to be an enjoyable day for you, Dana, and that has nothing to do with Tami or the proposal project, either."

Wordlessly, he communicated his intention to kiss her, giving her plenty of time to indicate she didn't want it. Instead, she linked her hands behind his neck, went up on her tiptoes, and kissed him. "See you in the morning, EHS."

Even Hotter Scott. Cal wore a crooked smile as he watched her saunter from Scoops with a spring in her steps and a sway in her hips. Then, because he always wanted the last word, he called out. "Can't wait, Dana Delicious."

Cal washed and dried her pots and tools, loaded her dishwasher, and then turned his attention to the three-gallon container of Rocky Mountain Road. After retrieving it from the freezer, he stirred the mixture using her slotted spoon. Nice and thick. Excellent.

The ring sat washed and waiting on a paper towel. Gently, he set it at the center of the round tub, then used a wooden spoon to submerge it two to three inches, about the depth of one scoop. After smoothing the surface, he covered the carton with its lid and returned it to the freezer to the particular spot Dana had cleared for it.

He was reaching for the handwritten "Do Not Disturb" Post-It note Dana had prepared when his phone rang. Caller ID flashed the name of the wide receiver for the Miami Dolphins. This was unusual. Cal seldom heard from Hank Anderson. That made Hank one of Cal's favorite clients. "Hello, Hank."

Cal listened for a minute, then thumped his head on the freezer door. Hank had so much talent, a natural athlete whose only limits on success were his personal demons. Eyes closed, voice tight, he asked, "So you're in jail where?"

He strode out of Scoops a short time later, his thoughts focused on the dumpster fire taking place in Texarkana involving his client, a sobriety slip, and a pushy paparazzo.

In an uncharacteristic miss for a detail man, Cal forgot all about the Do Not Disturb sign.

SEVEN

Dana ordered coffee to be delivered at six-thirty the next morning. She only felt a little bit guilty when she awoke snuggled beneath Angel's Rest's luxuriously soft sheets to the sound of a soft knock at the door. A muffled voice called, "Room service."

Five minutes later, wearing a luxurious Angel's Rest robe, Dana took a seat in front of the picture window with a view of Murphy Mountain. She held a delicious cup of coffee in her hand.

Dana told herself she wasn't taking advantage of Cal or Keefer Jennings by enjoying these perks of the job they'd hired her to perform. It didn't matter that the pitcher was a wealthy man who wouldn't think twice about the "expenses" she incurred. Dana wanted to *earn* the fee and the extras. She intended to offer Cal invaluable information and insight today —and ignore the buzz of sensual excitement created within her at the thought of spending an entire day with Cal doing romantic things.

Today was all about business. It had to be.

The task was going to be difficult. In addition to the

coffee Dana had ordered, room service had delivered a bottle of champagne and three dozen roses. Dana had found it way too easy to imagine Cal having sent them to her. Luckily, he'd included a card that reminded her of the purpose and kept her feet firmly on the ground. It read: *KJ needs to write something appropriately romantic on this card—Romantic gesture #1. Dana, please note the rose quality for me.*

Dana needed to keep the day humming along on an even keel, so she'd kept the champagne corked. At seven, she left her room and headed for the Angel's Rest spa for a blow-out, make-up, and mani-pedi.

She was almost giddy. It had been a long time since she'd been pampered, and she planned to enjoy every minute of it. She did precisely that and returned to her room to dress, feeling invigorated. And excited. Way more excited than she should be.

Ready a few minutes early, she grabbed the bottle of champagne and went downstairs, where she took a seat in one of the rockers on the front porch to wait for Cal's arrival.

His attention on his phone and a text he was sending, Cal didn't notice her at first. He looked harried, she thought. Tired. She called his name and added, "You look like you need a glass or twelve of this champagne. What's the matter? Has something happened?"

"Oh, hey Dana. Yes, I...whoa. Look at you. You look fabulous."

"Thank you." She'd thought the red jeans might be something Tami Styles might choose, and the white chambray shirt and multicolored vest had spoken to her. Celeste had helped her pick out the necklace and earrings after Dana declared she was going for 'mountain chic.' "It's not usually my look, but I think it works."

"It definitely works for me." He eyed the bottle of champagne longingly. "I could definitely use a drink. It's been quite the day already. I'll tell you about it in the car. I'll want to open that bottle at some point today. Need to taste test. For now, I'd better hold off on alcohol until I have food to go with it since I have mountain switchbacks to navigate. You're ready to go?"

"I am." She rose and picked up the champagne. "Where are we going?

"Up to a place near Heartache Falls for a picnic brunch."

Torn between delight and curiosity about what bothered him, Dana followed him to the Jeep he drove. He waited until they'd headed up into the mountains before beginning his story about his client's drunken public meltdown. "Anderson got into it with the photographer. He's lucky they charged him with battery rather than attempted murder."

"I'm sure it gets old being photographed everywhere you go."

"It's part of the job in professional athletics, especially for a first round draft pick. Hank is good people, but he needs to grow up. I spent hours calling in favors last night. Got him checked into rehab and with any luck, he'll have his head on straight by the time the season starts in August. But, enough about that. How was your room? Your spa date? Any feedback for me?"

"Everything is A plus. I've stayed at Angel's Rest a couple of times before, and it's only improved since then. The bed, the linens, the service—first class all the way. Tami and KJ shouldn't have any complaints about the night before the big day."

"Excellent. Any suggestions?"

She considered the question. "No. The champagne and flowers were a nice touch, and the pampering at the spa totally set the mood. I think you hit just the right amount of romance for the beginning of the day."

"Good. That's the plan."

Dana soon discovered that he'd managed to find a delightful place less than half an hour from town that she'd never before visited. "This is Mac and Ali Timberlake's yurt, isn't it? I've heard about it, but I've never seen it."

"Yes. It takes glamping to new heights. Apparently, the Timberlakes purchased a tent owned by a legit mountain man and added on. Substantially."

She exited the car and turned in a slow three-sixty. "What a view."

"Wait until you see the picnic spot. It's this way." He casually took her hand as he led her into a stand of aspen along a well-trodden path. In the woods, sunlight beaming through the canopy of leaves above them dappled the forest floor. Smelling crisp and clean, a gentle breeze whistled through the trees. So peaceful, Dana thought.

Walking deeper into the woods, she slowly became aware of a distant roar. Heartache Falls.

Her heartbeat accelerated, a combination of anticipation and altitude and exercise, she figured. They topped an incline, emerged from the trees, and Dana's breath caught. Heartache Falls stood in front of them, a frothy plunge of white water and rainbows glinting in the mist. She'd seen the falls from the viewing spot below but never from this high. It was private land. She spied a sunshine yellow blanket spread atop a bed of summer green grass surrounded by pink and white wildflowers. Champagne chilled in a silver bucket. Two large pillows and a giant picnic basket sat atop the blanket.

"I guess we're not worried about bears?"

"I asked Mac about that. We timed the picnic basket arrival carefully. Ali dropped it off less than ten minutes ago."

"Ali made the basket?" Dana's anticipation ratcheted up a notch. Ali was the original chef and originator of the recipes used at The Yellow Kitchen.

"Yes."

"Oh, Cal. Good job." They both took seats on the blanket. He set about popping the champagne cork. Dana dove into the picnic basket and discovered a feast.

They started with champagne and berries. Cal took a small spiral notebook and pen from his pocket and asked Dana for her criticisms and suggestions. She had to search to find any. "Maybe add the option of music? Personally, I think nature does the best job in that respect, but my viewpoint is far from universal."

"Good idea." He jotted a note. "Let me say that I agree with you. To me, the sound that water makes is one of the most beautiful music that exists."

"And, there's lots of variety. The roar of this waterfall. The crash of waves against a rocky beach. The bubble and rush of a creek and the gentle lap of the surf on a sandy beach." Grinning, Dana took a bite of a plump, juicy strawberry and added, "The drip from a leaky faucet."

Cal laughed. "Okay, maybe not all the sounds."

The conversation continued around nature during the rest of their meal. After they finished, they rose and strolled in companionable silence along the path running parallel to the cliff's edge that offered differing views of the waterfall. Eventually, Cal checked the time. "We should probably be going. The next stop on the proposal project involves an appointment."

"It does? What is it?"

"We have a private lesson in ornament-making with Gabi Brogan at her glass studio."

"Oh. Another excellent idea, Cal. I've done that before, and it's a lot of fun. Plus, KJ and Tami will have a keepsake to remember the day."

The session at the glass studio was a blast, and Dana knew she'd treasure the large, emerald green-and-gold teardrop ornament she'd made at Cal's side.

The next stop on their day of romance was the handmade soap shop named Heavenscents, where Cal had made arrangements for Dana to concoct a custom scent for lotions and soap. He'd even arranged for custom labels for the packaging.

"This was inspired," Dana told him as she sniffed the body lotion she'd created. "It's a very sensual experience, packaged perfectly for Instagram."

"I'm glad you think so. These creative stops aren't necessarily my idea of what makes a perfect pop-the-question day, but then, I would never propose to a social media influencer."

Dana was too curious not to ask. "What sort of woman do you see yourself with long-term?"

"For the longest time, I wasn't in a place where settling down felt possible, what with being on the road constantly and then on call 24-7. It didn't seem fair to commit to someone when I was rarely available. But recently, my perspective on things has started to change."."

How recently? Dana silently wondered.

"I'll admit that it feels like something's been missing from my life." He gave her a sidelong look and a mysterious grin. "As far as what I'd look for in a woman, well, I'd want someone who has a good heart, is a good friend, is honest and trustworthy and genuine. I've learned I'm attracted to the entrepreneurial spirit." He paused, and his grin went wicked. "A luscious set of legs doesn't hurt anything, either."

Savannah Turner interrupted the conversation at that point when she emerged from the shop's workroom, saying, "I have your bath oil and bubble bath ready. That's a fabulous combination of scents, Dana. I knew your taste buds were spot on because of the ice cream you create, but you really have a great nose, too. Don't you agree, Cal?"

"I do, but I'll admit I'm more partial to her mouth." Proving his point, he leaned down and kissed her.

Savannah fanned her face. "Oooh, it's getting hot in here."

"I guess that means it's time to cool off," Cal replied. "You ready for some ice cream, lass?"

"Already? I don't get dinner?" She'd been dreaming about the Yellow Kitchen's Bolognese.

Cal scooped up her Heavenscents shopping bag along with the one from Whimsies that held their ornaments. "You'll get dinner, don't worry."

"It's only two o'clock."

"I know. I'll explain on the way to Scoops. So far, we're right on schedule." He thanked Savannah for her help with his project and requested a minor change next time. "The bride is allergic to lavender, so I'd like to lose that particular essential oil at the main event."

"Not a problem. Thanks for including Heavenscents, Cal. I'm excited to be part of it, and I can't wait to find out the identities of the mystery couple."

"It was a lot of fun," Dana called as Cal ushered her toward the door.

Outside, he again took Dana's hand as they strolled toward her ice cream parlor. "Here's the deal, Dana. I'll admit I'm uncertain about the afternoon schedule. Shall I fill you in and get your input and ruin the surprise aspect of the day or proceed as planned?"

"Go ahead and tell me. I promise knowing won't ruin a thing for me."

"Okay. Before KJ lobbed his ice-creamed ring grenade into my plans, I had the proposal as the culmination of the date after dinner and dancing."

Dana perked up. "Dancing? Where?"

"Out at the Callahan place on Hummingbird Lake. Jackson is hooking us up with musicians. I figured dinner at the Yellow Kitchen, then dancing beneath the stars."

"Oh, yes! There are a dozen perfect spots for a marriage proposal at the Callahan's North Forty. He could do it beside the lake or on the dance floor, or in one of the treehouses. Have you seen the treehouses, Cal? They're spectacular."

"I have. I agree. The plan was to go to Scoops at this point in the afternoon, then head out to the lake to go sailing. KJ is a lake rat from way back, so he knows how to handle a boat. I figured it'll be time for a meal after boating. Unfortunately, the Yellow Kitchen is a no-go. They already have a twenty-fifth-anniversary party booked on July seventeenth. However, Ali Timberlake agreed to man the pots and pans at the North Forty kitchen."

"So, Ali is fixing brunch and dinner? That's quite a coup. She retired from personally operating the Yellow Kitchen's kitchen a few years ago."

"So I understand." His mouth twisted in a wry grin. "It took a significant donation to one of the local charities, but she's on board. It makes no sense for KJ and Tami to return to town after dinner for an ice cream cone for dessert. Plus, if they ran late, you'd need to keep Scoops open. When I analyzed things, I realized that a midday proposal would probably suit the bride just fine. I've arranged for a camera crew to capture everything from the Rocky Mountain Road reveal forward. If Tami wants, she can go live and let her fans experience the engagement right along with her."

"Oh, Cal. That's brilliant. I think that totally will appeal to @TamiStyles4U."

"So, we're a go for the special cone?"

"We are."

"Which of your friends did you choose to be the "bride?""

"I decided to go with someone young," said Dana. "Holly Montgomery is Lucca Romano's stepdaughter. She's in her mid-twenties and works across the street from Scoops."

"At the Mocha Moose. I've met her. A really nice young woman."

"I think she'll be excited to find the ring and not touchy about being used as a test bride. Just to be clear, I checked with her mother and got Hope's okay."

"Excellent."

"Want me to go ahead and call her, or should I wait until we're all set up?"

"Well, we're five minutes from Scoops. Maybe give her a call and ask her to come over in fifteen?"

Dana nodded and made the phone call. Holly promised to be there, and as they walked the final block to Scoops, Dana returned to something he'd mentioned a few moments ago. "You said that soap making and glass blowing weren't your ideas of what makes a perfect pop-the-question day. What is?"

"Spontaneity. I know elaborate proposals like this one is the thing these days, but I'm not a fan of staged events. To me, asking a woman to be my wife should be a private, personal moment for the two of us."

"I like the way you think, Buchanan." Dana felt precisely the same way. Then, a new thought occurred to her. "What social media do you use?"

"Sometimes I'll post on the sports message boards affiliated with my university, but beyond that, I don't have a presence anywhere."

"Seriously? I figured with your job, you'd need it."

"My agency employs a social media manager for each athlete we represent. If something needs my attention, the manager lets me know. Otherwise, I remain unplugged from social media."

"Okay, that's it. I need to call Holly and tell her not to visit Scoops."

"Why?"

"Because I'm handing the Rocky Mountain Road with real rocks to you. We share the same social media philosophy. You are my unicorn in the dating sea. Will you marry me, Cal?"

He shot her an unreadable look. "Well, maybe not quite this spontaneous."

Dana laughed and looped her arm through his. "Oh, well. It was worth a try."

They arrived at Scoops in good spirits. Business was brisk, but Dana's competent assistant manager and weekend crew had the situation under control, just as Dana had expected. She checked the time as she headed into the back. Five minutes before Holly was due to arrive. Just enough time to don her apron and deposit the special Rocky Mountain Road container into the case.

She grabbed her Scoops apron and slipped it on. Having followed her into the back of the shop, Cal reached for her apron strings and tied them at her back. "Would you get the ice cream from the freezer while I wash my hands?"

Dana moved to her work sink and switched on the water as Cal strode toward the freezer. He opened the door and stepped inside. A moment later, she heard a muffled curse.

"Um, Dana?" His tone was level, but tight.

"Yes?"

"The shelf is empty. The carton isn't where I left it last night."

EIGHT

CAL DIDN'T PANIC. NOT REALLY. "DID YOU HAVE SOMEONE move it?"

"Move it?" Dana said, her voice a squeak. "The Rocky Mountain Road?"

"Yes."

"No! No one was supposed to touch it. It's not there?"

"It's not where I put it last night."

"Caramel fudge butter pecan!" Dana rushed into the freezer. Standing beside Cal, she pointed an accusing finger at the Do Not Disturb note attached to a rack. "Calum, why is that note exactly where I left it?"

Cal cursed using the actual words. "I forgot all about that. My client called from jail just as I started to slap the note on the carton. I totally got distracted."

"Okay. It's probably no big deal." Dana turned and left the freezer. Cal followed on her heels. "We had two-thirds of a carton of Rocky Mountain Road in the case when I left last night. I can't believe we went through that much today, but stranger things have happened."

She hurried to the front of the store. Her smile tight,

Dana walked directly to the display case. Cal's stomach sank at her frown. He eyed the spot in the freezer case where Rocky Mountain Road always sat. The carton was about three-quarters empty. "It's my third most popular flavor. The amount left is what I would expect from a normal sales day."

Her head jerked up to meet Cal's, her big brown eyes stricken. "This isn't the container."

Cal still didn't panic, but he winced. "Any ideas what could have happened to it?"

Dana, however, panicked. She dashed back to the freezer, where she flung open the door and rushed inside, searching frantically among the containers. "It has to be here. You must be mistaken about where you put it. Where did you put it, Calum?"

"In that empty slot on the shelf." Even as he said, he mentally retraced his steps. He'd been distracted by the phone call, but he distinctly remembered shutting the freezer. He was ninety-nine percent certain that he'd put it where he'd indicated.

"That can't be! It has to be here." She rifled through the stacks of ice cream cartons, then stopped herself and started over methodically.

Cal sure didn't see it. "I'm going to double-check the display case."

It wasn't there. None of the employees had seen it. Dana joined Cal in the front of the shop, her complexion drained as white as Avanillalanch.

"We must have been robbed. Quick, call Sheriff Turner! What are we going to do? Will my insurance cover the ring? Oh, dear. What will that do to my premiums?"

"Dana. Dana. Dana." Cal took hold of her by the shoulders. "Calm down. It'll be okay. We will find it. Somebody knows what happened to it. The ice cream fairies didn't raid your freezer overnight."

"Well, somebody did!"

"Speaking of somebody, where's my brother?"

Dana stilled, then glanced around the shop. "Rusk. Yes, he should be on shift." Addressing her assistant manager, she asked, "Stephanie? Where's Rusk?"

"He left on his lunch break a few minutes before you arrived, Dana."

Cal asked, "Where did he go?"

"Was he carrying anything when he left?" Dana added.

"He left through the back, so I don't know if he carried anything. He didn't say where he was going."

"But he opened for you this morning, didn't he?" Cal asked Dana. "Was he by himself?"

"Until eleven, yes."

"Okay then." Cal pulled his phone from his pocket and placed a call to his brother. It went to voicemail, which was no big surprise because Cal had seen Rusk's phone on the kitchen counter this morning when he made coffee. His brother was unusual for someone his age in that he wasn't tethered to his screens. Cal envied him for that. He recorded a voicemail asking Rusk to call him ASAP and followed that with a text.

Looking at Dana and her crew, he asked, "Any guesses where he went for lunch?"

"No," a teenaged girl said. "But Rusk did mention that he might take a little more than his hour because he had an errand to run."

"Great," Dana muttered.

"No hints as to what this errand is?"

The teen shook her head. To Dana, Cal said, "We can stay here and wait for him, or we can go looking. Your call."

"Let's look. I can't stand around twiddling my thumbs. I'll go crazy."

Cal gave her shoulder a comforting squeeze. "Don't fret so, Dana. This is my responsibility. If it's gone, it's gone."

The teenager asked, "What is so important about a tub of ice cream?"

Tears flooded Dana's eyes as she opened her mouth. Cal responded. "It's sentimental. I helped make it. It's my first batch." To Dana, he said, "Let's go."

They tried the Mocha Moose, Murphy's Pub, and Rusk's garage apartment in case he'd gone home for his fav PB&J. Seeing his brother's phone on the kitchen counter at the same spot where it sat earlier this morning strongly suggested to Cal that Rusk had not been by.

And yet, no one they'd asked recalled seeing him today. "His truck isn't here," Cal said as they left the apartment. "I didn't notice it around Scoops anywhere, did you?"

"No."

"Well…." He checked his watch. "His lunch hour is almost up. We could drive the streets one time and then head back to Scoops. Sound like a plan?"

Dana nodded. As she climbed into his passenger seat, he decided to be methodical about the search and drive the grid, four avenues by eight streets. "You watch to the right. I've got the left."

They went up Aspen Street and down Spruce, keeping their eyes sharp. Despite his attention, Cal darned near missed it. The very last place he expected to see his brother's vehicle parked was the lot in front of Eternity Springs' retirement home and assisted-living center. Cal slammed on his brake. "There he is."

"At the retirement home? Why is he at the retirement home?"

"Haven't a clue. Let's find out." He parked, and they walked inside.

Just past the front desk, the large community room was filled with people. Celeste Blessing stood at the front of the room with a microphone in her hand. As Cal scanned the crowded room for his brother, he tuned in to Celeste's monologue.

"...such a fun exercise. Thank you all for your enthusiastic participation. Linda, if you'll make sure everyone has a slip of paper and a pen to vote in the runoff, please?"

A woman wearing a name tag began walking from table to table, dispensing the requested items. Celeste continued, "So, without further ado, allow me to announce our top three vote-getters in our renaming contest. Votes will be counted during this afternoon's festivities, and the winner will be announced at the conclusion. Ladies and gentlemen, the three highest-scoring votes for the new name for our wonderful new facility are Eternity's Edge Retirement Village, Angels Not Ready To Rest Senior Living Center, and Young At Heart Senior Home."

A spate of applause interrupted her. When it died down, she continued. "Now, onto what brought us all here together this afternoon. Happy 70th Anniversary to John and Leslie Mills! I believe John—or as he's known around here, CrackerJack has a few words he wants to say?"

A frail elderly man rose from a seat at a table at the front and used a cane for support as he turned to face the gathering. Behind John Mills, Rusk stood in a doorway to what appeared to be the kitchen. Cal leaned close to Dana and murmured, "There's Rusk."

Cal could see no way to get to his brother without walking through the middle of the gathering. Dana must have identified the same problem because she said, "Let's wait until after this gentleman speaks."

"Thank you, Celeste," John Mills said, his voice surprisingly strong coming from that frail body. "Thank you all for joining us this afternoon. I won't keep you long from our cake and ice cream, but I want to say a few words publicly to my blushing bride."

"Ice cream!" Dana murmured, elbowing Cal in the ribs.

He nodded. It now seemed evident that Rusk had taken the carton of Rocky Mountain Road to bring here to the senior facility. Cal would bet a hundred dollars that he'd also brought along vanilla. He and Dana hadn't checked the status of other flavors in the freezer.

At the front, John said, "Sweetheart. Love of my life. Seventy years ago, you stood beside me in that little chapel in Denver and vowed to be mine. We've shared most of the whole kit-n-kaboodle—the better and worse, richer and poorer, sickness and health. I pray that when we get to the death do us part, part, the good Lord takes me first. I'm selfish that way. Anyway, throughout it all, you never faltered. You honored your vows to me even when I didn't deserve it. I want you to know that I'd been saving up to get you something special for this anniversary since it's extra special to you."

He took his gaze away from his wife long enough to show the gathering a grin that still had a bit of wicked in it to explain. "She made a bet with her sister the day before our wedding that we'd see seventy years or more together as man and wife. My Leslie hates to lose a bet."

He returned his attention to his wife. "Sadly, the fire that took our house last winter got my money box, too, so those earrings I've been wanting for you literally went up in smoke."

"That's okay, honey," Leslie Mills said. "It's the thought that counts."

"I knew you'd say that, so I didn't worry too much about it. I couldn't get you something sparkly, but I did manage something else I know you love. And when I thought about it, I decided it suits the occasion better than a bauble. So, when I finish yapping, this youngster over here is gonna scoop you up a double-dip cone of your favorite, Rocky Mountain Road."

"Oh, John," Leslie said. "How sweet!"

"We've had a bit of a Rocky Mountain road this past year, my love, but that's behind us. I have it on good authority— none other than Ms. Celeste's—that life is gonna be smooth as homemade ice cream for us for the next little while. So, that's what I've wanted to say. I love you, Les. A man couldn't ask for a better wife and partner in life. I've been saying this ever since my buddies in the oilfield hung the nickname on me. If I am the Crackerjack, then you are without a doubt the prize. Happy anniversary."

He walked over to his wife, slowly leaned down, and kissed her. The room erupted in applause. John Mills called out. "Cake and ice cream for everybody. My treat in honor of my prize of seventy years!"

Dana clasped her hand to her chest. "That's the sweetest thing I've ever seen."

Yes, it was. Crackerjack Mills reminded him of his own maternal grandfather. William Reece had been loyal, responsible, and a principled man of his word. He'd adored his children and grandchildren, but his love for his wife, Cal's Nana, had been the thing of legends. Cal had loved his grandparents with every fiber of his being. They used to joke about the gifts Cal would buy for them when he signed a professional baseball contract. Sadly, William Reece had passed right before Cal got called up to the majors. One of Cal's biggest regrets was that he'd never been able to buy his Papa that Lamborghini.

That regret was what caused Cal to look at Dana and say, "I'll make it up to you, I promise."

NINE

"EXCUSE ME?" DANA ASKED.

Celeste carried a big sheet cake out of the kitchen toward the head table where John and Leslie sat. Cal didn't respond, and she didn't pursue the question because they both spied Rusk and started forward through the crowd.

Cal's brother pushed a cart that held cartons of ice cream, a stack of cones, and a stack of bowls, spoons, cake plates, and forks into the community room. Spying three full cartons —Rocky Mountain Road, Avanillalanch, and Royal Gorgeous Gumdrop, if she wasn't mistaken—Dana drew her first easy breath since discovering the missing container.

They'd made it in time!

Right on Cal's heels, she said, "Oh, my heavens. We cut that close. Thank goodness Rusk hasn't already dished up the ice cream! Wasn't that the sweetest declaration of love ever?"

"One of them," Cal murmured.

At the front of the room, Celeste asked that residents remained seated and explained that the treats would be served at their tables. "Our young Scots friend, Rusk Buchanan, will be around to take your order for ice cream."

Cal and Dana reached the Mills' table just as Rusk picked up an ice cream scoop. Upon noting their arrival, Rusk arched his brows in a silent question. Cal answered by clasping his brother's shoulder and giving it a squeeze with his left hand. With his right, he smoothly plucked the ice cream scoop from Rusk's possession, saying, "I've got this."

He turned a bright, warm smile upon Leslie Mills. "Happy anniversary, Mrs. Mills. Seventy years! You are an inspiration to us all."

"Thank you, dear. Do I know you?"

"No, ma'am, I haven't had the pleasure. My name is Calum Buchanan, and I'm here to serve you up the ice cream your husband ordered for you. We have your favorite Rocky Mountain Road and…." He glanced down at the other two cartons, frowned, then up at his brother, the question in his eyes.

Simultaneously, Rusk and Dana repeated the flavor names.

Cal asked Leslie Mills, "So, cone or cup?"

"I'll have a cone, please. Scoops makes the very best sugar cones. One dip of Rocky Mountain Road."

"Nuts or sugar sprinkles?"

"I like mine naked," she said, giving him a saucy wink.

Cal laughed. "Don't we all."

Dana didn't take her gaze off the ice cream scoop as he made a shallow dip in the requested flavor. He dipped a second time, then met Dana's gaze and nodded. Her shoulders slumped with relief.

Had she not paid such close attention, she would have missed what happened next. Using sleight of hand worthy of a pickpocket, Cal dropped something sparkly into the ice cream container, then he buried it into a big, fat scoop of Rocky Mountain Road which he plopped onto a sugarcone.

Dana's jaw dropped as Cal handed Leslie Mills her cone.

He said, "Promise me you'll be careful when you eat this, and remember, Crackerjack, here, *always* delivers the prize."

Leslie Mills might be elderly, but she hadn't lost any mental faculties. She knew something was up. She shifted a bright, inquisitive gaze between Cal and her husband. John Mills shrugged.

"John, how about you?" Cal asked. "Want to pick your poison?" But even while he made the query, Cal was scooping up another serving of Rocky Mountain Road. This time, from the center of the carton. He topped a cone with the ice cream and handed it to Dana with a wink. "Don't choke on it, lass."

She glanced down at the cone and spied a telltale band of metal. *Whew. Success.*

So, what had Calum put in Mrs. Mills' ice cream? Dana was dying to find out.

Celeste cut the cake, and one of the spryer residents volunteered to pass them out. Dana clandestinely deposited the engagement ring in a napkin and slid it safely into her pocket. At the same time, Cal asked John and Leslie to share the story of their wedding day. They were cute about it, teasing one another and telling a tale of financial hardship and family resistance. "So, you eloped?" Dana asked, caught up in the tale.

"We did." Leslie Mills smiled like a cat with a saucer of cream. "Our parents wanted me to marry John's brother. He was the elder and due to inherit the business, but John won my heart."

"Aww," Dana said. "That's so sweet."

Leslie took another bite of ice cream and…bingo. She lowered the cone and stared at it with wide eyes. "What in the world?"

She plucked something from the cone. Green and gold. An emerald earring? "Oh, John. You didn't!"

"I didn't!" He looked confused.

"He did," Cal corrected, and as smoothly as he'd acquired the ice cream scoop from his brother moments ago, he plucked the item from Leslie Mill's hand. Dana realized he'd had a cleansing wipe ready and waiting because he quickly had the familiar earring sparkling. Dana had noticed the pair in Silver and Sparkles Jewelry the day they bought the engagement ring.

Cal handed the earring and its mate, fresh from his pocket, over to Leslie, saying, "Your husband's love for you inspired an Eternity Springs angel."

While the anniversary couple shared a kiss, Dana softly asked Cal, "Why?"

He shrugged and gave a boyish grin. "Because I can."

Dana's heart melted to mush even as she wondered how he'd come to have those earrings on his person. For whom had he purchased it and why? She couldn't wait to find out.

They remained at the anniversary party until the cake and ice cream had been consumed, and the winning name was announced. Then, as the Buchanan brothers ate their ice cream, Cal explained events to Rusk. In turn, his brother relayed how John had paid a visit to Scoops early that morning and ordered the ice cream. "Pretty lame-brained of you not to tag the carton," Rusk told Cal.

"Maybe." Cal watched the anniversary couple with his arms folded across his chest, a faint smile upon his face. "I think it all worked out quite nicely. Sometimes, things happen for a reason." He turned to Dana and asked, "You ready to continue our project?"

She blinked. "It's still on?"

"Of course. What happened here didn't change anything.

If anything, it proved the value of doing a practice run. So, how does a sailboat ride sound?"

"Wonderful. Simply wonderful."

She waited until they were outside the newly christened Young At Heart Senior Home to hand over the engagement ring. Then, as he tucked it away into a pocket, she asked him about the earrings.

"It's kind of a long story," Cal replied. "How about I share while we're on the water?"

Dana muffled her impatience, and she answered his questions about the retirement home during the fifteen-minute drive to the marina on Hummingbird Lake.

Cal handled the boat like a master. They talked sports and music and a little politics before she again broached the subject of the jewelry. "I was hoping you'd forget," he responded.

"Seriously? Surely by now, you know me better than that."

"I do." He gave an exaggerated sigh, then flashed her a grin. "Let me tell you about my granddad. Has Rusk told you anything about our family?"

"A little. I know that your mother is an American and your father, a Scot. You grew up in Scotland but spent summers in the States. You moved here to play baseball when you were in high school."

"Sarasota, Florida, to be exact. My grandparents retired there. I lived with them all through high school and college. My granddad was my hero." He told her of a Korean War hero, a loving helpmate to a wife crippled with rheumatoid arthritis. Cal spoke of the support his grandfather had given his baseball dream and of the lessons William Reece taught and the values he had instilled in Cal.

"That upbringing served me in good stead when faced

with all the excesses a successful professional baseball career put within my reach. I loved Papa deeply. How John Mills spoke about his wife today reminds me of my grandfather. Since I've been in Eternity Springs, more than one person has told me that it's a little piece of heaven, a place where angels make special things happen. I saw a chance to be part of it, so I acted. I like thinking that what happened today with the ring was meant to happen."

"That's very nice, Cal. You were the Mills's angel today. But I want to know the rest of the story. How is it that you just happened to have beautiful emerald earrings in your pocket? You bought them from Amy, didn't you?"

He heaved a heavy sigh. "I was hoping to distract you from that. But, yes, I bought them from Amy. My intention was to give the earrings to you. I thought they suited you."

"What?" Dana's heart went thud-a-thump. "Why?"

"As a thank you for all you've done for me and this project. I planned to give them to you at the end of this test run. But look, I don't want you to feel let down. I'm sure Silver and Sparkles will be able to hook me up with something else just as nice."

For me! He bought those earrings for me! An entire flock of butterflies took flight inside her stomach. She had to clear her throat to speak past the lump of emotion that blocked it to say, "Let down! Don't be silly. Cal, I don't need a gift. You're paying me a mint to help out in addition to all the perks. Hello, room service and spa appointments."

"That's separate. That's business. This was personal." Holding her gaze, he added, "Honestly, it's never been strictly business with you, Dana D."

With that comment, the air between them took an intimate turn. Dana licked her lips and said, "Not for me, either."

Heat fired in his eyes, and he reached for her. Dana lifted

her face for his kiss just as a wind gust caught the sail, interrupting the moment and forcing Cal to turn his attention to the boat. They didn't speak for the next twenty minutes while he sailed to the next proposal plan stop—the Callahan family's luxurious compound.

He docked the sailboat half an hour before sunset. Ordinarily, this time of year, at least part of the clan would be in residence, but with everyone in Texas for a family wedding, they had the place to themselves.

Sexual tension hummed in the air between them as they sampled wine and hors d'oeuvres while watching the sun paint the sky crimson and gold above a sapphire Hummingbird Lake. Afterward, they walked hand-in-hand to the dining room, where they finally opened the room service bottle of champagne and dined on Ali Timberlake's glorious lasagna. Their conversation grew serious as Cal spoke about his career-ending injury, and Dana shared the story of her failed relationship with her ex. As the evening progressed, neither Cal nor Dana made mention of Keefer Jennings's prospective engagement.

For something that wasn't a date, it sure felt like a date to Dana. The best date of her life!

Cal never once brought out his notebook to take notes.

After dinner, they slow danced to the sound of a saxophone played by a musician Cal had brought down from Aspen. Cal held her close, his hand drifting slowly up and down her spine.

At nine p.m., he led her up to the rooftop deck of one of the elaborate treehouses Brick Callahan had built on the property. Propped up against pillows, Cal held her as fireworks exploded over Hummingbird Lake. "This is a slimmed down version of the real deal. I wanted to test the equipment and see how the special shapes I ordered for the grand finale looks."

When a flurry of pink, white, and red hearts burst against the dark sky and signaled the end of the show, Dana sighed and said, "Oh, Calum. This was simply spectacular. You get an A-plus for romance."

His voice was a low, rough rumble. "Do I?"

"You absolutely do."

"I'm glad you think so." He dragged his thumb up and down her arm. "Okay, then. I declare proposal project practice officially over. I figure if KJ can't figure out where to take it from here, there's no hope for him."

Dana shivered at his touch. "I have to agree with you on that."

He shifted their positions. Light from a three-quarter moon and a million stars softly illuminated his features as he stared into her eyes. "There's a question I've been waiting for the right moment to ask, Dana D."

Just kiss me. Please, just kiss me! she thought. "What is it, Cal?"

"It's about your remodeling plans."

"My...what? My remodeling plans!" *He thinks about home renovation at a time like this? What happened to Mr. Romance?*

"Yes, your remodeling plans. Any chance I'll get that tour when I take you home tonight? You gonna show me your upstairs, lass?"

Oh. Oh! Dana wanted to whimper, but she valiantly fought it back and found a lighthearted tone. "Well, EHS. I suspect a private tour could be arranged. Why don't you take me home, and we'll find out."

TEN

THE FOLLOWING MORNING, CAL SENT KJ THE PROPOSAL practice video and received an enthusiastic approval from the pitcher. Then an emergency with another one of his clients took Cal away from Eternity Springs. He phoned Dana each evening and managed to squeeze in a quick visit over the Fourth of July weekend. As they lay together in her bedroom after setting off some fireworks of their own, he asked her about the For Sale sign he'd noticed in the window at the Mocha Moose.

"Yes, Scott Ferguson put it up on Wednesday. He and his wife are moving to Florida to live with Scott's mother, who is elderly and needs help. They're keeping their home here but hope to sell the coffee shop by summer's end. Scott told me they're ready to be snowbirds."

"Have they gotten any interest in the business?"

"Not that I've heard, but it's not a worry for them. If the Fergusons are ready to leave and no one has made an offer, Celeste will buy it. That's how she rolls."

"Hmm." He dragged his thumb lazily up and down her arm.

Dana pressed a kiss against his bare chest. "So, is KJ all ready for the big day?"

"I think so."

"I'm a little concerned. Have you been keeping up with Tami's social media?"

"No, I haven't." Cal's voice held a rueful note as he added, "I've had my hands full of narcissistic crybaby athletes, I'm afraid."

"You don't sound as if you're thrilled with your job these days."

"I'm not. So, what has @TamiStyles4U been up to?"

"She's not been in the best mood lately. Her posts have taken on a snarky tone. I admit I'm worried about the project." Dana went up on her elbow and met Cal's gaze. "What if she doesn't like Eternity Springs? What if the day of romance doesn't check all of her boxes? What if—heaven help me—Tami doesn't like my Rocky Mountain Road? All that influence could backfire on the town and on Scoops. We could be canceled!"

"Now now, lass." Warm amusement lit his mesmerizing green eyes. "Don't fret. I don't believe that will happen, but you should know me well enough to be confident that I have a plan for that."

"You do?"

"I do." He rolled her onto her back and rose above her. Then, staring down with a wicked grin, he said, "I am the plan man."

He took her breath away when he kissed her, igniting their passion once more. Later, much later, Dana addressed his plan man comment. "The Even Hotter Scot with a plan. Am I a lucky girl or what?"

The big day finally arrived. Cal set up his operations center in the back of Scoops, where he and Dana waited for reports from their observers in the field. Not that they really needed them. Tami had already gone public about her romantic weekend with her "honey," and her social media supplied everything Dana and Cal needed to know. The only thing she'd kept quiet about was the actual name of what she called Quaintsburg Springs.

"I guess Tami doesn't want paparazzi or fans disturbing their trip," Dana observed. She showed Cal an Instagram post of the picnic at Heartache Falls. "Tami calls it Heartsoar Falls. So we won't get the publicity we expected after all."

Cal shook his head. "No. Don't think that for a minute. I don't doubt that internet sleuths already have the name. We will have photographers in town before dark. The fact that it'll take that long for them to arrive is part of the reason I initially chose Eternity Springs. KJ and Tami will get their privacy, and you and the other merchants will get your publicity. It'll be a win for everyone. Trust me."

"I do. I'm still nervous. I think I'll go work the front for a bit as a distraction." Her expression fierce, she added, "Promise you will guard the freezer with your life."

"Scouts honor," he replied, holding up his hand in the traditional salute.

"You're wearing your World Series ring today," Dana observed.

"Yes." He lowered his hand and looked down at the ring. "I figured representing Team Bling today was appropriate."

"Makes sense." Dana gazed at his large hand and recalled how she'd awakened with it cupping her naked breast as he'd slept. "Were you ever a Boy Scout, Buchanan? Do they even have scouts in Scotland?"

Cal leaned in and gave her a kiss. "We absolutely have Scot Scouts. Say that fast five times. Unfortunately, I had to quit when I was nine. Scouts interfered with baseball."

With a nod, she turned and headed for the front of the ice cream parlor. At the door, she stopped. "With your life, Calum."

"Don't worry, love. The ring is safe. It's not going missing again. It's more important to me than you realize."

It was a curious comment, but an update from Whimsies noting the couple's arrival for their ornament-making session distracted Dana from the subject. She spent the next hour visiting with customers and dipping up cones. Business was brisk today, and Rusk was in full flirt mode. The exercise relaxed her and reminded her of what was important.

What's the worst that could happen? @TamiStyles4U could bash her Rocky Mountain Road online. But Dana and Scoops would survive that. She had confidence in her product, business, and core customer base. Scoops would be fine.

She'd paid off her banknote on Thursday. She had the Buchanan boys to thank for that. She had nothing whatsoever about which to worry. Well, except for the fact that with the proposal project behind him, would Cal ever find a reason to visit Eternity Springs?

Me. I'm the reason. Cal likes me.

Cal Buchanan wasn't the type to have a woman in every port, so to speak. It's true they hadn't talked about the future after today, but he'd given her no reason to believe that she'd never see him again. Rusk wasn't leaving town for another three weeks. Cal might return to Eternity Springs to see his brother.

He'll come back to see me. He likes me.

Dana liked him, too. Very, very much.

Maybe he'd waited to say anything about the future because she'd been upfront about wanting to take things slow. He knew this was her first relationship since the painful breakup with a longtime lover. She hadn't been ready to talk about the future herself until, well, now. Cal Buchanan knew how to read a room.

Well, she should broach the subject herself. That's what one did in honest relationships.

Honestly, she didn't want him to disappear. She liked Calum Buchanan. Okay, she more than liked him. She was pretty sure she loved him. How's that for lightning speed?

Whoa, okay. That thought frightened Dana even more than the idea of @TamiStyles4u dissing her Rocky Mountain Road.

Dana was still a little shaky due to the love revelation twenty minutes later when Cal emerged from the back and said he was going out on an errand.

"What? You can't leave. Our, um, special guests could arrive at any time!"

"They haven't wrapped things up at Whimsies yet. I'll be back in plenty of time."

"Where are you going!"

He flashed her a grin. "Go guard the freezer, lass."

She set her teeth and growled, then turned on her heel and hurried to the back. Cal had been teasing her about the freezer, she knew, but she intended to guard it anyway.

He'd been gone fifteen minutes when she received her text from Gabi stating that KJ and Tami had left Whimsies and were headed her way. Dana's mouth went dry, her pulse rate rose. She fanned her face with her hand and cursed her Even Hotter Scot with one of her favorite strings of words. "That peanut butter caramel crunch nougat."

She immediately texted him using all caps. THEY ARE ON THEIR WAY!

Fifteen long, stressful seconds later, he texted back. *So am I. All is well.*

"Yeah, right," she muttered before ducking into the

restroom to check her hair and freshen her lipstick. Then she removed the special carton from the freezer and carried it to the case. At that point, Rusk was the only server working. Meeting his gaze, she pointed toward the Rocky Mountain Road. "Touch that and die."

His lips twitched with a grin. "What if someone orders it?"

She pointed to the carton she'd just removed from the case and set on the side counter. "Use that."

"Aye aye, Captain." Rusk gave her a salute as the door chimed, and Cal strode inside.

Dana glared at him. "Well, glad you could make it."

"Had a bit of business I needed to take care of." He had a sparkle in his eyes and wore a mysterious grin as he took hold of Dana's waist, lifted her, and twirled her around.

"Calum!" She protested. "What do you think you are doing?"

"Celebrating. Hoping you'll celebrate with me."

He danced her through the swinging door into Scoops back room as Dana said, "We don't have time to celebrate. KJ is on his way."

"KJ can wait." Then he took her mouth in a kiss hot enough to melt all the ice cream in Scoops.

Totally lost in the moment, Dana failed to hear the jangle of the doorbell announcing new customers. She only came back to the present when Rusk opened the door and said, "Dana, I really could use some help out here to dish up some Rocky Mountain Road."

"Oh. Oh! Cal. They're here!"

"Go do your thing, lass," he told her, his voice a sensuous purr. "We will continue this celebration later."

"Okay. Okay. Do I look all right?" She smoothed her hair.

"You look gorgeous. Lipstick's a little mussed." He

swiped his thumb across her lips. "There. That's better. I'll watch through the window and be out as soon as my presence can't tip her off."

"Okay. Good." She hurried toward the door but hesitated when she reached it. Then, looking back over her shoulder, she asked, "What are we celebrating?"

"Later. It's game time. Go throw your best pitch."

Dana nodded, braced herself, pasted on a smile, and pushed through the door into the parlor. Upon getting a good look at the starry-eyed couple, her nervousness evaporated. Cal's day of romance obviously had been a success. "Welcome to Scoops. How can I help you today?"

Keefer Jennings tore his besotted gaze away from his girl. "My lady here will have one dip of my favorite flavor, Rocky Mountain Road, in a cone. Her favorite flavor is peach, so I'll have a double-dip cone of Pikes Peach."

"Now, that's sweet," Dana said.

"It's important to know the one you love," said the all-star.

"That is so true. Now, if you will take a seat at the table in front of the window, I'll bring your ice cream cones right over."

They did as she asked, which framed them perfectly for the prepositioned hidden camera. She nodded to Rusk to start the video while she quickly and efficiently prepared the cones.

Moments later, Dana handed a single dip cone of Rocky Mountain Road, complete with sprinkles and sparkle, to @TamiStyles4U. Her squeal a short time later rattled the windows.

ELEVEN

CAL TIMED HIS ENTRANCE INTO THE FRONT OF SCOOPS FOR when Keefer Jennings went down on one knee to make it official. He was there to swoop up the abandoned cones and hand them off to his brother before things got messy and to offer to clean the ring before KJ placed it on Tami's finger.

In reality, Cal quickly and surreptitiously switched the ice-cream smeared ring with a clean, sparkling, Instagram-ready duplicate.

Well, "duplicate" wasn't the proper term. The dirty ring was the Amy Elkins designed setting that Dana had favored, the one she'd said she'd wear in a heartbeat. It sported a Colorado Rock just a little bit bigger than the one Cal's client gave to his bride-to-be. The stones to each side were classic and classy, just like Dana.

After sending the video of the big moment to both KJ and Tami's phones, Cal worked to usher the pair along their way to the next stop on the romance tour. Events had totally stopped service inside of Scoops. The line now stretched beyond the front door, and he knew he wouldn't get Dana to himself until her customers were satisfied.

Cal wanted some satisfaction. He wanted to whisk Dana away to somewhere private and convince her to say the words he believed he'd seen hovering on her tongue. He wanted to hear that his instincts weren't out of whack.

Once the lovebirds were out the door, Cal pitched in behind the display cases to whittle down the crowd faster. Once the rush was over, he turned to Dana and said, "Come with me, Dana D. We have a new project to discuss."

"We do? Another project? So soon? Something to do with the Mocha Moose?"

"Come with me and see."

She turned to Rusk. "Can you cover for me, Rusk?"

"I can. I will." From the corner of his mouth, he added, "Otherwise, my brother might beat me up."

"Let me go get my purse."

When Dana disappeared into the back of the parlor, Rusk gave his older brother a knowing look and asked, "So what are you going to do with that extra engagement ring?"

"I have an idea. It just needs a little more time to perk."

Dana was looking at her phone as she joined the Buchanan brothers a few moments later. "Look! Eternity Springs and Scoops are both trending! And it's good trending, not bad trending."

"Told you so," Cal smugly replied.

He escorted her to his car and opened the passenger door for her. Once she'd taken her seat, he leaned down and kissed her before shutting the door. Cal slid into the driver's seat and started the car.

Focused on her phone, Dana didn't ask where he was taking her to discuss the new project. Instead, she read aloud posts and responses on Tami Styles' social media. "Wow. That ring photographs spectacularly. How in the world did you get it so clean, so fast?"

"Trade secrets," Cal answered.

She laughed, then returned her attention to her phone and continued to share her social media reactions.

Cal was glad they didn't have far to drive. He had trouble keeping his gaze on the road. Dana bubbled with excitement and sparkled with joy. She was the loveliest thing he had seen in forever.

Only when he pulled into the Angel's Rest resort entrance did her attention shift away from the screen. "You've brought us here? Do we have a meeting with Celeste to discuss this new project?"

"No. Beyond making the arrangements I requested, Celeste has nothing to do with this."

Dana's brows winged up. "You're making me curious."

"I'm hungry."

"Oh. So, we're going to the Bistro? That works for me. I'm hungry, too. I was too nervous to eat lunch."

"Glad to hear that," he murmured beneath his breath.

Celeste's golf cart was waiting for them just like he'd asked. But rather than steering toward the restaurant in the resort's main building, he headed for a picnic spot along an isolated section of Angel Creek. Dana's curiosity was evident, but she held her questions.

He found everything just as he'd ordered. A picnic basket sat atop a quilt made in shades of blue and gold. Champagne chilled in a bucket, and two fishing poles waited baited and ready for casting. "We're going fishing?"

"If we so desire. I thought we might need to relax after the tension of the day. Few things are as relaxing as throwing a fly into the water."

Dana very deliberately put away her phone. "I like the way you think, Buchanan."

"I'm counting on that."

He opened and poured the champagne while Dana unpacked the picnic basket, setting out meats, cheeses, and nuts. She waited until he'd handed her a glass to ask, "So, what are we celebrating?"

Suddenly, Calum was nervous, worse than he'd been before walking onto the field for the seventh game of the Series. Was he making a mistake here? Was he ready for such a significant change? He set down his champagne and picked up a fishing pole and...yeah.

That said it all, didn't it?

Forget the champagne lifestyle. He was ready to fish. And if he read the signs right, he already had a catch on the line. Now, he just had to land her.

He licked his lips and tossed his line. "We are celebrating my new venture. When I went out today, I signed some papers. You are looking at the new owner of the Mocha Moose."

Dana's eyes went round. "What?"

"I bought the Mocha Moose."

"I thought for a minute you might. Someone with your resources is probably always looking for investment property. I hope whoever you get to run it maintains the quality of the coffee served."

"I will. Personally. I'm going to operate it myself."

Slowly, she set down her glass and rose to her feet. "How can you do that? You live in Atlanta."

"I thought I'd move to Eternity Springs."

Dana didn't jump with joy and clap her hands. She didn't squeal with delight. Cal's stomach did a nervous flip when instead, she carefully picked up the fishing rod and tossed the line. Then, after a full minute of silence, she asked, "Are you serious, Calum Buchanan?"

"As a ring buried in Rocky Road," he returned, reeling in

his line.

"Why?"

He made another cast. "Well, it seemed like it was meant to be. I'm told that happens quite often here in Eternity Springs. The fact is that I'm a coffee snob. I've been roasting my own beans for a few years now and experimenting with different blends. I think I have a product the townspeople will enjoy. Also, I enjoyed working the counter at Scoops and interacting with the public. I think running the Mocha Moose will be right up my alley.

"So, what do you think? Is it a good idea?"

"I think...I don't understand. You are a professional baseball player—"

"Former."

"—and a sports agent. Not a barista, Cal. Why would you want to do this?"

Okay. Well, this is it. Cal set down the fishing pole. It had served its purpose and settled his nerves. His customary confidence was back. Approaching Dana, he removed the fishing pole from her hand and set it aside. He took both her hands in his, stared down into her eyes, and spoke from his heart.

"Because I love Eternity Springs. And, I love you, too."

As warm emotion melted into Dana's beautiful brown eyes, Cal went down on one knee. He reached into his pocket and pulled out the ring. Classy, classic, and smudged with ice cream. Just like the woman of his dreams. "Dana Delaney, would you marry me?"

She steepled her hands over her mouth. "Oh, Cal. Wow. I don't...I do...I can't...I want...this has happened so fast!"

"I know it has. But when you know, you know. And I know. This is the life I want. You are the woman I want to share this life with. We don't have to rush to the altar. I'm good with a longish engagement if you're more comfortable with that."

"Yes."

"Yes, you'll marry me? Yes, you'd be more comfortable with a long engagement? Yes, I can stand up now because I'm kneeling on a rock?"

Laughing, she said, "Yes, all of the above."

"Thank God."

Cal rose to his feet and Dana threw her arms around his neck and tugged his mouth to hers for a kiss filled with joy, excitement, and passion. When she attempted to end the kiss, Cal, being Cal, refused to release her and turned up the heat. They were both breathing heavily when they finally came up for air.

Her gaze soft and warm, Dana lifted her hand to cup his cheek. "This *has* happened so fast, but we're not teenagers. I know, too. I know my own heart. I love you, Calum Buchanan. I do want to marry you, and I've always dreamed of being a June bride. Would that work for you?"

"Next June?" When she nodded, he declared, "Absolutely."

"I'm thrilled you're moving to Eternity Springs. I can't wait to walk into the Mocha Moose to bum a cup of coffee from you each morning."

"I'll charge you in kisses. Then after lunch, I'll saunter over for a taste of afternoon delight at Scoops."

Her eyes twinkled. "We don't have a flavor called Afternoon Delight."

"I have a recipe." He waggled his brows at her.

"I just bet you do." Dana wrapped her arms around Cal's middle and gave him a hug. "What a fabulous day this has been."

"Well, today's not over yet." Suddenly in a hurry, Cal

pulled away from Dana and began tossing food into the picnic basket. One couldn't leave charcuterie lying around in bear country. "Grab the champagne, would you, please? Hurry."

Dana laughed, her tone bubbly as the wine. "Is there a fire?"

"Definitely. Most definitely." He ushered her into the golf cart and spun the tires as they took off. Luckily, their destination was only two minutes away. When he braked in front of the isolated cottage, Dana's brows arched, and her tone was incredulous when she asked, "Here?"

He'd brought her to Angel's Rest's famous Honeymoon Cottage.

"It's research for the next project."

"What project?"

"The honeymoon plan." Cal leaped from the golf cart and went around the front to extend his hand toward Dana. "You know me, I like to do my research. How can I plan the best honeymoon ever if I've not researched the matter thoroughly?"

"The honeymoon plan," Dana murmured. "I like it."

"No, you're gonna love it." Cal all but ran up the front walk, tugging her along with him. Once they were inside and the door shut behind them, he scooped the champagne bucket from her hands and set it down on a nearby table. Then, swooping her up into his arms, he carried her back to the bedroom, where everything waited just as he'd ordered.

Dana spied the serving cart placed beside the bed, and her lips twitched with a smile. Brown eyes sparkling, she asked, "What's this?"

"My fantasy. I've been thinking about it since the day I opened the door to you and your Pike's Peach."

"I hope you ordered chocolate sauce."

"I did." He lay her down on the mattress. "And caramel. Nuts. Candy sprinkles, too."

"Excellent." Dana licked her lips, grasped his shirt, and tugged him down on top of her. She nipped his earlobe and declared, "Because I intend to have myself an Even Hotter Scot sundae."

THE CHRISTMAS PAWDCAST

An excerpt

Chapter One

Dallas, Texas

"Carol of the Bells" drifted from the sound system and blended with the laughter of the holiday party guests who were taking their leave. Mary Landry worked to keep the smile on her face as she hugged and cheek-kissed and waved goodbyes to the stragglers. She had enjoyed the party, and she was thrilled that so many invited guests had attended. But seriously, would these people never go home? She still had so much to do! How could it possibly already be December twentieth?

"Tonight was so much fun," bubbled a wedding planner from Plano, her blue eyes sparkling with champagne. "Landry and Lawrence Catering throws the best party of the season, year in and year out. Thanks so much for inviting us!"

"I'm so glad you could join us." Mary graciously accepted the woman's enthusiastic hug and glanced up at her date. "Shall I call an Uber for y'all?"

"We're good," he said. "I'm the designated driver tonight, but I can't say I missed the booze. Your non-alcoholic eggnog was killer."

"Mary is the best chef in Dallas," the wedding planner declared. "Restaurants are always trying to lure her into their kitchens."

"Mary! Great party!" A venue manager sailed toward

them, which helped ease the first couple out the door. "I don't know what tweak you made to your mac-and-cheese recipe, but it made the exquisite simply divine."

She hadn't changed a thing. "Thank you, Liz."

"You gonna share your recipe?"

"Nope. Trade secrets."

"Dang it. Although my waistline and arteries both thank you for that. Merry Christmas, Mary."

"Merry Christmas."

Finally, almost an hour after the party had been scheduled to end, Mary's business partner Eliza Lawrence shut the door behind the last guest. She gave her long brown hair a toss and flourished her arms like a game show hostess. "We are so freaking awesome!"

Mary laughed. "Yes, we are."

"I do believe tonight even topped last year's party, which I didn't think would be possible."

"Everything went like clockwork—except getting guests to depart."

Eliza waved her hand dismissively. "That's the sign of a successful event. You know that."

Mary nodded. It was why their Christmas event was the one party of the year where Eliza, the logistics director of their business, loosened her timeline.

"Everyone raved about the food as usual," Eliza continued, "but the shrimp balls were a particular hit. You outdid yourself with those, Mary. The vendors who were here tonight are going to talk them up to their clients. We'll be up to our elbows in shrimp all next year."

"I figured they'd be a hit. Nothing has topped my maple mac-and-cheese, though. I think that was all gone by nine o'clock."

"The Landry and Lawrence classic." Eliza sighed happily.

"You ready for a glass of champagne? I built time for champagne into our schedule. The cleanup crew doesn't arrive for forty minutes."

"I'm more than ready." Mary's thoughts returned to her to-do list, and she winced. "Mind drinking it in my office? I need to finish my dad's gift before I head home tonight."

Eliza chastised her with a look.

"I know. I know."

Her partner reached out and gave Mary a quick hug. "I'll grab a bottle and glasses and meet you in your office on one condition."

Mary's mouth twisted in a crooked smile. "What's that?"

"Change your clothes before you break out the hot glue gun. I don't want to be taking you to the ER with third-degree boob burns five days before Christmas."

Mary snorted.

"I think I heard almost as many comments on how great you looked tonight as I heard about how fantastic the shrimp balls tasted. It's a spectacular dress, Mar. I'm glad you decided to show off your curves for a change. Emerald is your color. It brings out your eyes. I swear, when Travis arrived and got a look at you, I thought he was going to swallow his tongue."

"Because I'm wearing last year's Christmas gift." Mary fingered the teardrop garnet pendant that nestled against her breasts. "He accidentally left it off the list of things he asked me to return when he dumped me."

Eliza wrinkled her nose. "If I said it once, I said it a thousand times. The man is a dewsh. I know we couldn't cut him from the guest list because he does own three wedding venues in the Metroplex, but I honestly didn't think he'd have the nerve to show up with her in tow."

"Oh, I knew they'd be here." That's why she'd made such an effort with her outfit tonight.

"Well, you definitely won tonight's skirmish. Raylene sailed in here dressed in her slinky silver sequins, holding her nose in the air and flashing her rock, but you put her in her place without so much as a 'Bless your heart,' just by being gracious."

"She's a beautiful woman."

"And you're a natural red-headed pagan goddess—who will find somebody worthy of you. Trust me, you dodged a bullet by getting rid of that creep."

Emotion closed Mary's throat, and tears stung her eyes. How was it that Eliza always knew just the right thing to say? While she'd put Travis Trent behind her, and she hadn't cried over him in over five months, seeing him tonight hadn't been easy. No woman enjoyed seeing her ex parade her replacement around in front of her. Especially not in her own place of business. Clearing her throat, Mary tried to lighten the subject by saying, "I was aiming for sexy Santa's helper."

"Honey, I wouldn't be surprised to find a dozen men in red suits and white beards lined up outside our door when we leave here tonight."

Mary laughed. What would she do without her best friend? "Oh, Eliza. I do love you."

"I love you, too. Now go cover up that fabulous rack so you can finish your dad's gift. I'm going to change, too, and then I'll grab the bubbly and meet you in your office."

Ten minutes later, armed with a hot glue gun and wearing jeans, a sweatshirt, and her favorite sneakers, Mary put the finishing touches on the Daddy-Daughter scrapbook she'd made for her father. It had long been a Landry family tradition between her parents and two siblings to exchange handmade gifts at

Christmas. With her brother and sister both married, the practice had expanded to include spouses and Mary's two nephews and three nieces. Of course, she bought the little ones toys, too, but handmade gifts where the ones that mattered for the adults.

Eliza strolled into her office, carrying two crystal flutes in her right hand and a green bottle in her left. She set the glasses on Mary's desk and went about the business of opening the champagne. "Sorry I took so long. John called to grovel about missing the party, so I let him do it even though I totally support his job. I knew what I was in for when I fell for an obstetrician."

"Did his patient have her babies?"

"She did. Mama and triplets are doing great."

"Excellent."

Eliza filled two glasses with the sparkling wine, handed one to Mary, then raised her glass in a toast. "Merry Christmas, BFF."

"Merry Christmas. I hope you and John have a fabulous time in Hawaii."

"How can we not? Ten days of sun and sand, just the two of us, totally unplugged? It'll be heaven."

"The unplugged part sounds like heaven," Mary agreed.

"You're such a traditionalist, Mary."

"And unapologetic about it. For me, Christmas wouldn't be Christmas without all the trappings. I want family around me, bubble lights on the tree, and carols on the sound system. I want cookies to decorate and big fluffy bows on gifts. I want midnight mass and hot apple cider and 'It's a Wonderful Life' and sleigh rides. And I want snow!"

Eliza clinked her glass with Mary's. "And this is the difference between a girl born and raised in south Texas and one who grew up in the Rocky Mountains. So, when are you planning to leave for Colorado?"

"With any luck, first thing tomorrow morning." Mary sipped her champagne, then set it down. She checked the finishing touch on the scrapbook with her fingertip. The miniature fishing creel placed at the corner of a twenty-year-old photo of her father fishing with his three children in Rocky Mountain National Park was nice and dry. It was safe to close the book. Mary needed to wrap it and the two hardcover novels containing the handmade gift IOU's she was giving her brother and sister before she headed home. Her sibs understood her busy season and would be happy with better-late-than-never, thank goodness.

"In other good news, I finally found a dog sitter for Angel. Jason Elliott told me tonight he'd take her. He just needs to clear it with his roommate. He said he'd call me tonight if there was a problem, and my phone hasn't rung."

On cue, Mary's cell phone rang.

It lay pushed to the side of her desk in its seasonal decorative Santa case. Her ring tone of choice for December was "White Christmas," and for the first time in Mary's life, the sound of Bing Crosby's voice didn't make her happy. She closed her eyes and whimpered a little as she reached to answer. "Hello?"

Two and a half minutes later, she disconnected the call, buried her head in her hands, and groaned.

Eliza set a champagne flute in front of her. "No room at Jason's inn, either, I take it?"

"No. Jason was my last hope. There's no other option. I've called every vet, every boarding facility, pet hotel, and pet sitter within fifty miles. Everything is full and has a waitlist. Nobody is offering me any hope that Angel will find a bed for Christmas."

Eliza winced. She took a sip of her drink and then pursed her lips and pondered a moment. "You asked Sarah?"

"Yes. And Linda, April, José, Kiley, Kenisha, Sam, Father Tom, Reverend Jenkins, Officer Larimer..."

"The butcher, the baker, and the candlestick maker?"

"Them, too."

"I'm sorry, sweets. You'd know I'd help if John and I weren't leaving for Hawaii tomorrow. I suppose it wouldn't be kind of me to say I told you so when you said yes to Wags and Walks?"

Mary chastised her partner with a look.

Eliza lifted her champagne in a toast. "Honey, you know I love dogs as much as anybody, and I think the work you do for Wags and Walks Rescue qualifies you for sainthood. But that dog..."

"She's an angel," Mary defended. "She's aptly named."

"Unfortunately, people aren't any different about choosing their pets than they are about choosing their partners. I'm afraid you might be stuck with that dog for a long time. Appearance matters. Note that you didn't choose to name her "Beauty" when the other volunteer pulled her from the pound and then dumped her on you at the last minute."

Mary brought her chin up. "Beauty is in the eyes of the beholder. Angel's forever family will see past her...challenges...to her sweet personality. I simply haven't had time to find them. Besides, it's not like I didn't know that I was taking on a special case when I let Rhonda Blankenship leave her with me."

"I know. I know. But I also witnessed your call to the rescue director. I heard her swear on her mother's grave that she would find a dog sitter over Christmas if you agreed to step in for Rhonda and take the new dog."

Mary shrugged. "Things happen."

"Right. And women elope and bail on commitments at the

last minute all the time. So where did Rhonda and her new husband move to again?"

"Yap. It's an island in the South Pacific. It's supposed to be beautiful."

Eliza rolled her eyes and drawled, "I hope they'll be very happy. So that's it, then? You have no choice but to take that poor, pitiful, diarrhetic dog with you on a fourteen-hour car trip, then foist her off on your parents for two weeks? They're going to love that."

"They won't mind. Much. They're both dog lovers, although Mom does prefer little dogs."

"Nothing about Angel is little. She's a horse. A big, hairy horse."

"She's a big dog, yes, but don't forget she's carrying extra weight."

"I don't see how, considering that she tosses her cookies every time she eats. Oh, Mary. I'm going to worry about your road-warrioring in a seen-better-days Ford uphill through the blizzard with only a big, ugly, sick dog for company."

Mary gave her friend a chastising look. "Number one, my car might have a lot of miles, but it runs like a champ. Number two, I'm going to pretend I didn't hear the U-word. Number three, I've checked the travel conditions between Dallas and Eternity Springs, and nobody is predicting a blizzard to hit in the next two days. It's two to four inches of snow at the most once I reach the mountains, and I'll most likely be home before it starts. Number four, Angel isn't sick. The pregnancy has given her a sensitive digestive system. And finally, number five, I forbid you to spend one minute thinking about me, much less worrying. I expect you to devote all your time and attention to wringing every bit of comfort and joy from your romantic Christmas vacation with

Dr. Hottie. And, to assist in that endeavor, I have a little something for you."

Mary opened one of her desk drawers and removed the small, wrapped package she'd placed there earlier.

"Mary!" Eliza exclaimed. "We already exchanged gifts. I love, love, love, love the organizer you gave me."

"I'm glad. This is a little something extra. It's my heart gift."

Eliza's eyes widened. Her voice held a note of wonder as she accepted the box, saying, "But…you didn't have time this year. You've only just finished your dad's gift. You're giving your siblings IOU's. You didn't even have time for the big fat family tradition event that's so important to you, your 'Gift of Giving to a Stranger.' But you took the time to make something for me?"

Mary could have pointed out how Eliza never failed to be there for her during the breakup with Travis. She could have talked about their excellent working relationship or the way Eliza always made her laugh when Mary really needed a laugh. But instead, she simply said, "You're my best friend, Eliza."

Her best friend burst out in uncharacteristic tears and tore into her present. "Booties! You knitted booties for me!"

"For the plane ride."

"Because I always kick my shoes off, and my feet always freeze. They're so soft. They're like a turquoise cloud. They're perfect. Thank you, Mary. I love them." Eliza threw her arms around her friend and gave her a hard hug. "There's only one problem. No way I won't think about you when I'm wearing them."

"Fair enough. You have permission to think about me only while you're sitting in First Class, wearing my booties, and sipping a Mai Tai."

"It's a deal. I'll drink a toast to you and Angel and tap my turquoise heels three times and wish you safely home over the river and through the woods without encountering a tornado or a blizzard or a cat named Toto."

"No cats. Angel doesn't care for cats."

Both women turned at the sound of the loading dock's buzzer. The cleanup crew had arrived. Eliza took one last sip of her champagne and set down the flute. "I've got the after-party. Consider it my heart gift to you. Stay here and wrap your presents, then go home and get a good night's sleep so that you and Angel can get an early start in the morning."

Mary accepted the gift in the spirit it was offered, and she gave her friend one more hug. "Thank you. Merry Christmas, Eliza."

"Merry Christmas, Mary." Booties in hand and whistling "I Saw Mommy Kissing Santa Claus," she left the office. A minute later, she ducked back inside and tossed something toward Mary, saying, "Since you're so big on Christmas traditions, I think you should stick this in your purse."

Jingle bells jangled as Mary caught the red ribbon holding the sprig of mistletoe that had been part of their decoration.

Eliza said, "You want to be the Girl Scout Elf when you're out walking Angel and run into Santa Hunk. Always prepared, you know."

"Santa Hunk?

"I know you are spending Christmas in a small, isolated town with a shortage of single guys, but hey, it's the season of miracles, right? Put it in your purse, Mary."

Mary laughed, did as she was told, then returned to her gift wrapping. She finished up quickly. After checking with her partner, who assured her that everything was under control, she headed home to bed.

Mary dreamed vividly that night. Snow swirled in peppermint scented air, but there were no clouds in the inky blue sky, only a full moon and a million stars. She was flying. She was flying in a sleigh pulled by reindeer—with Angel in Rudolf's lead position. Angel's nose glowed red, and around her neck hung a St. Bernard's cask of brandy. Bing Crosby crooned about a white Christmas from the sleigh's sound system speakers.

Mary wore her green Christmas party dress, a red felt hat with jingle bells and pointed tip, and sparkling Judy Garland ruby slippers with curled, pointy toes. Was the curl because they were elf shoes, or because mistletoe hung above the sleigh, and Santa Hunk had kissed her all across the Pacific?

When the sleigh sailed past an airliner headed toward Hawaii, she came up for air long enough to give Eliza a beauty queen wave. Eliza lifted her Mai Tai in a toast.

Mary awoke with a smile on her face.

As a rule, she wasn't one to put any stock in the notion that dreams foretold the future. Still, right before she backed her loaded-up eight-year-old Ford Explorer out of the driveway, she added a new song to her playlist for the trip.

Mary Landry headed home to Eternity Springs, Colorado, for Christmas, singing along to "Santa Baby."

LUKE

BOOK ONE OF THE CALLAHAN BROTHERS
TRILOGY

An Excerpt

Maddie Kincaid was in trouble. Again.

Trouble caused by a man. Again.

Maybe she should reconsider the convent idea after all.

"There's the sign, Oscar," she said to the fat goldfish swimming in the clear glass fishbowl belted into the mini-van's passenger seat to her right. "The Caddo Bayou Marina. We made it."

The goldfish didn't answer, although the way her world had changed in the last twenty-four hours, Maddie wouldn't have been surprised if Oscar had leapt from the water and belted out "The Yellow Rose of Texas."

Approaching the marina entrance, Maddie gently applied the brakes and flicked her left-turn indicator. Since beginning this long, meandering trip to southwestern Louisiana fourteen hours ago, she'd taken extra care to obey all traffic laws.

It wouldn't do to get pulled over by the highway patrol, not when she had four million dollars' worth of an illegal substance stacked between her dry cleaning and a new sponge mop.

Gravel crunched beneath the minivan's tires as she drove across the lot and claimed a spot between a Dodge pickup and a Chevy Suburban. After shifting into park, she took a deep, calming breath and twisted the ignition key. The engine sputtered and then died. In the sudden quiet, Maddie let out a soft, semi-hysterical laugh. *Better it than me.*

She sat without moving for a full minute. Her mouth was dry, her pulse rapid. She needed to use the facilities. "Okay," she murmured. "We made it. We handled the crisis. Got here in one piece. We did good. Now we'll have help."

Help. From the DEA. "I must be out of my ever-lovin' mind."

Maddie opened her car door and stepped outside. The summer morning air was hot, heavy, and thick with moisture. She glanced toward the boat slips, then back at the marina's ship store and restaurant. "I'll be right back," she said to Oscar as she grabbed her purse before shutting the door. Then, noting the heat and imagining boiled goldfish, she reconsidered. Moments later, fishbowl cradled in one arm, purse hanging from the other, she headed for the store and its bathroom.

As she walked toward the building, movement at the gas dock out on the water caught her notice. Three pontoon boats filled with people dressed in swim trunks and brightly colored clothing motored slowly away from the dock. *Must be one of the swamp tours she'd seen advertised on a billboard on the way in,* Maddie surmised. Her gaze drifted over the crowd before it snagged on the man standing at the stern of the trailing boat as he stripped off a sweat-stained T-shirt and tossed it away. He lifted his arm above his head to take a minnow bucket off a hook, and Maddie sucked in a breath.

My, oh my, oh my.

She may be tired, scared, hungry, thirsty, and ready to wet her pants, but abs like those deserved a second look—even if she had sworn off studly men forever.

He wore a battered straw cowboy hat, low-riding Hawaiian-print swim trunks, and grungy deck shoes. Sunglasses hung from a cord around his neck, and a sheen of sweat glistened on his deeply tanned skin. His body looked lean and hard, with long legs and shoulders as broad as the Mississippi.

Yum

Her appreciative gaze lingered until a good look at his face made her forget about his form. Even from a distance, she could see devastation etched in his expression. Empathy melted through her. Poor man. She wondered what had happened to him.

Then, as if he tangibly felt her gaze, he jerked his stare away from the minnow bucket dangling from his hand and met her gaze head-on. His eyes narrowed, his jaw hardened. He straightened, squared his shoulders, and widened his stance, his aggressive posture a challenge to her for catching him in a private moment.

Whoa. Maddie gave a tentative smile and took a step back. *In another moment, he'd be baring his teeth like a wolf,* she thought.

A wolf in low-riding swim trunks.

"Oh, for crying out loud," she muttered, deliberately turning away, shifting the fishbowl from one arm to the other. What was wrong with her, ogling a bayou boy when she should be looking over her shoulder for drug-dealing killers? Had she totally lost her mind?

Yes, she was afraid so. This was what an overload of stress and lack of sleep did to a girl.

Dismissing the party barges, Maddie redirected her attention toward the ship store. The place appeared deserted. In fact, other than the pontoon boats now disappearing from view, the only signs of life around the entire marina were a pair of big black grackles pecking at the ground near a lidded metal Dumpster.

Cautious in ways she'd never been before, Maddie slowed her steps and took a second look around.

On the murky water of the bayou, dozens of boats floated beneath the shelter of covered docks. Both the gas pump on the water and the one near the cement launch ramp remained unmanned. She spied an open tackle box and two fishing poles propped against a silver propane tank, but the fishermen themselves were nowhere to be found.

Curious. On a Saturday morning, she'd expect the marina to be bustling, especially on a warm, windless day. Apprehensive now, Maddie advanced toward the ship store's door.

A handwritten sign was taped to the glass at eye level. "Closed for funeral," she read aloud. "Reopen at 1:00 p.m."

Well, that explained the quiet, and all the vehicles in the lot probably belonged to the swamp-tour people. It didn't solve her need for a bathroom, however, so Maddie turned toward the boat slips in search of the *Miss Behavin' II*.

The woman she'd come to see lived on a houseboat moored at this marina. It shouldn't be difficult to find. If Terri Winston wasn't aboard, then Maddie would backtrack to the fast food restaurant she'd passed on the interstate. She hoped it didn't come to that. She felt safer here in this out-of-the-way spot than she did in a town or on the highway.

It had occurred to her as she drove through central Texas at three o'clock in the morning that the Brazos Bend police could have issued a BOLO for her van. From that moment on, she'd lived in fear of seeing the red-and-blue flash of a highway patrol car.

Maddie noted two normal-sized houseboats and one huge houseboat that brought the *Queen Mary* to mind among the twenty or so boats berthed in the slips. Since the mansion-boat didn't seem like something a federal agent would own, she made her way toward the smaller vessels.

The name painted across the stem of the first read *Playtime*. Maddie's stomach knotted with tension as she approached the second. It'd be just her luck for Ms. Winston to have up and moved her boat.

"Bayou Queen," she read aloud, grimacing. She blew out a heavy sigh, then gazed at the floating palace. It had to be eighty feet long, with front and rear decks, outdoor ceiling fans, and a spiral staircase to the roof with its fiberglass flybridge and swim slide. A boat like that would be called *Bellagio* or *Shangri-la*. Not *Miss Behavin'*.

Since she was out of other options, she decided to be thorough. To her shock and relief, the sign hanging from the rear deck of the mansion-boat displayed the words she prayed she'd see.

However, the *Miss Behavin' II* appeared as deserted as the rest of the marina.

"Hello?" Maddie called. "Ms. Winston? Is anybody home?"

She heard nothing but the squeak of a rubber boat fender against the wooden dock in reply.

Maddie grimaced. Where could the agent be this time of day? At the funeral? A quick check of her watch left Maddie moaning. If Terri Winston was at the funeral and the funeral lasted all morning, it didn't bode well for Maddie's bladder.

Her teeth tugged at her lower lip and she groaned aloud. Had she made one more mistake in a long line of them by putting her life in the hands of a stranger based solely on the advice of that meddler Branch Callahan? So what if Branch insisted that Terri Winston was a stand-up woman who'd listen to Maddie's story without immediately snapping on the handcuffs? Recent events suggested that Brazos Bend's leading citizen wasn't as knowledgeable as he claimed.

Branch hadn't known about the drug ring operating right under his nose, had he?

Maddie let out a long, shaky sigh. She may well have made a serious mistake, but what other choice had she had? Despite her vow of self-sufficiency in the wake of the disaster that had been her love life, she'd needed help. When she'd swallowed her pride and reached out to her father, he'd been off indulging in one of his new hobbies— wildlife photography in the Alaskan wilderness. According to his latest assistant—his latest twenty-year-old, starry-eyed bed partner, no doubt—he'd be beyond cell phone reach for another week —an eternity to someone in Maddie's predicament.

A predicament growing more dire by the second. She needed a bathroom *now.* Raising her voice, she tried again. "Hello? Ms. Winston?"

Nothing.

Maddie glanced from the houseboat to her van, then back to the floating manse. It was a long way back to that fast food place. Not a soul was in sight. Even if she tripped an alarm, she'd probably have time to visit the restroom and make herself scarce before anyone showed up to investigate. "Ordinarily I wouldn't think of trespassing," she told Oscar. "But these are no ordinary times."

Besides, Ms. Winston was a woman. She'd understand.

Maddie wiped her sweaty hands on her shorts and then stepped onto the boat and tried the sliding glass door. It slid open easily, and when no alarm sounded, she stuck her head inside, gazing with interest at the luxurious features and furnishings. She hadn't seen a boat this tricked out since she visited her father for a week aboard a Greek tycoon's yacht. "Ms. Winston?" she called. "Terri?"

No response.

Maddie stepped inside. An overstuffed couch and two plump easy chairs faced a plasma TV hanging on a wood-paneled wall finished with crown molding. A wraparound bar separated the main living area from a kitchen complete with granite countertops and a Sub-Zero refrigerator. She spied recessed lighting, brass hardware on the cabinets, and roman shades and padded cornice boards on the windows.

"Wouldn't Daddy love to have one of these," she murmured.

Maddie set Oscar and her purse atop a stylish iron and glass dining table, then made a beeline for the bathroom. With personal business out of the way and fully intending to return to the dock to wait for Terri Winston like a polite unin-vited guest, she nevertheless paused when she passed the refrigerator.

She *was* awfully thirsty. Maddie tapped her foot, then sighed. At this point, what was one more sin?

She opened the fridge. Hmm... the agent must have recently visited the grocery store. Lots of meat, cheese, eggs. Looked to be a Paleo dieter except for the three gallons of low-fat milk. She spied a twelve-pack of spring water and a six-pack of imported beer. Maddie reached for the water, but somehow, her hand grabbed the beer.

Boldly, she rummaged through Ms. Winston's galley drawers to find a bottle opener and, after hesitating over a bag of Double Stuf Oreos, grabbed a half-empty package of pret-zels from her pantry. She sat at the table, drank her stolen beer, and finished off the bag of pilfered pretzels. When she belched aloud without even trying to smother the sound, Maddie knew she'd lost it.

"Maybe I'm having a heat stroke," she said to Oscar. Or a post-traumatic stress episode. But it couldn't be that. There was nothing at all "post" about this stress.

Something told her that murdering, drug-dealing dirty cops wouldn't give up the hunt for her just because she didn't go home last night.

Grabbing her beer, she tossed the empty pretzel bag into a plastic trash can, then walked past one, two, three bedrooms and another bathroom to the front deck. Maddie gazed out at the bayou, where late-morning sunlight strained through the thick green canopy of trees and vines that stretched across the murky water of the swamp. Long strands of Spanish moss dangled from the branches of the live oaks like gray-green tinsel, adding an eerie atmosphere to an already fantastical morning.

"I can't believe I'm in trouble again," she said softly. This time, she hadn't sought it. This time, she hadn't fallen for a seductive man's line. This time, all she'd done was clean house!

The urge to cry came over her then, but Maddie fiercely fought it back. She'd sworn off crying at the same time she'd sworn off studly men. She was stronger now. She'd survive this.

But as she returned to the kitchen to gather her purse and her pet, despite her best intentions, a pair of big, fat tears overflowed her eyes and slid slowly down her cheeks.

She swayed on her feet, overcome with exhaustion and emotion and the effects of half a bottle of dark ale. Then, channeling her inner Goldilocks, she chose a stateroom, kicked off her sneakers, found an out-of-the-way spot on the floor for Oscar, and crawled into a queen-sized bed.

≈

Luke Callahan set the plastic bottle of mustard on the ship store counter and said, "That ought to do it."

Perched like a heron atop a three-legged stool behind the counter, Marie Gauthier sighed heavily, her frown deepening the lines in skin tanned dark and leathery. "Ah, it be a sad day, *cher,*" she said, ringing up his purchases. "Me, I'll be missing that old coot. I thought the service was fine and fitting."

Luke nodded and cleared his throat. "Terry liked a good party."

"Mais yeah." Marie neatly stacked Luke's groceries in a brown paper bag. "That man, he loved a *fais do-do,* and he loved the bayou. It's the right place for his ashes to rest."

Luke agreed. Spreading Terry Winston's ashes was the single part of this god-awful day that had felt right.

"And now, what about you, *mon ami?* My man, he say you're taking the *Miss Behavin' II* away from Caddo Bayou. Are you leaving us for good? The ladies here, they will be brokenhearted."

"I'll be back." Luke lifted the grocery bag into his arms and offered her the first genuine smile he'd managed in a month. "I'm going fishing for a few weeks. One of my brothers just bought a new thirty-foot Grady-White. I'm meeting him in Lake Charles and we're heading out toward the Keys."

"An extended fishing trip? *Mon Dieu.* My man, he be pea green with envy when he hears that. So, it's true, then? You're trading in your gun and badge for a fishing pole and bait?"

Luke's smile slowly died as the sick sensation in his stomach returned. He'd broken the rules when he went after Terry's killer. He'd resigned before they could fire him.

"Beyond fishing for my supper for the next few weeks, I'm not sure what I'm going to do."

Marie Gauthier reached across the counter and gave Luke's arm a comforting pat. "Ah, it's none of my business, anyway. My Pierre, he always tells me I'm a nosy old woman. You take your time, *mon ami*. These are grievous wounds you've suffered. The bullets, they are bad enough, but losing your partner... That Terry, he was like a father to you. You give yourself time to heal, Luke. You come back to us when you're whole again."

When he was whole again. *Yeah, right.*

Luke tried to put the old woman's words out of his mind as he exited the store and made his way across the parking lot toward the wooden pier and the *Miss Behavin' II.* The day had been a killer, and he was anxious to put it behind him. He wasn't scheduled to meet Matt for two more days, but after the strain of Terry's send-off, Luke wanted some downtime, some time alone. Time to decompress.

The months of constant danger during the undercover assignment in Florida had worn him down. Saying good-bye to Terry Winston had nearly killed him.

He'd held up all right in the heat of the moment. The gunfight in the Miami warehouse, stealing the car, the mad race to the ER while trying to staunch Terry's wounds and his own. He'd even managed when, after fighting for weeks in the hospital, Terry had squeezed Luke's hand, and died.

It was the aftermath that did him in. The reality that Luke's mistake had gotten his partner and friend killed was a devastating burden to bear. He'd gone a little crazy bringing the killers to justice. It cost him his job, but he didn't regret it.

What he regretted was losing control of himself last night when Terry's friends set out to honor his memory in a way the man would have appreciated. Terry's farewell had started at sunset with a party the likes Caddo Bayou hadn't seen in years. Lots of food and drink, music and dancing.

Luke had kept it together until the band played a rendition of Jimmy Buffett's "Lovely Cruise." At that point, he'd sat down on a bench and bawled like a baby.

He'd hit the booze hard after that in a misguided attempt to dull the pain, and the rest of the night remained fuzzy in his memory. The festivities had continued past dawn, culminating in this morning's church service and the trip into the swamp to spread Terry's ashes. The remnants of a hangover still throbbed in Luke's head and the lack of sleep dulled his thinking.

A dog's bark jerked Luke back to the present, and his mouth twisted in a hint of a grin as the stray mutt who'd adopted him during the past week came bounding toward him from the woods where he'd been off exploring. A mix of golden retriever, boxer, and who-knew-what-else, the dog must have been dumped on the highway by an uncaring owner. The mutt had made his way to the marina the same day Luke returned to Caddo Bayou.

Luke had tossed the dog a bite of his burger, and from that moment on, the mutt considered himself Luke's. Luke took longer to come around to the idea, but finally, last night, he'd sealed the deal by giving the dog a name.

"Whoa, there, Knucklehead," Luke said as the dog went up on his hind legs, planted his front paws on Luke's shirt, and licked his face. Luke pushed the mutt off him, saying, "The slobber factor is getting out of hand. If you're going on this trip with me, you're gonna have to get some control."

His tail wagged, his tongue dangled out one side of his mouth, and he looked so stupidly friendly that Luke let out a laugh. He reached down and scratched the pooch behind the ears before continuing toward the *Miss Behavin' II*. The dog bounded aboard ahead of Luke, then waited at the door for Luke to let him inside. Like a flash, he disappeared toward the starboard stateroom where he'd claimed the queen-sized bed for his own.

As Luke stowed the last of his supplies for the upcoming fishing trip, he wondered why he'd been a sucker for the mangy hound. He hadn't had a pet in seventeen years. A man in Luke's business had no business owning a dog. Since his job was eighty-five percent travel, he couldn't properly care for a pet.

"Well, that's not a problem anymore, is it?" Luke slammed the cabinet shut with more force than necessary. He didn't want to think about the job. He didn't want to think about what he was supposed to do with the rest of his life. He hadn't felt this lost since the day his father booted his butt out of Brazos Bend.

Well, he didn't have to think about any of that now. For the next three weeks, he'd think of nothing more serious than which bait to attach to his line. Old Marie Gauthier was right. He needed time. He'd give himself time. That's exactly what Terry would have told him to do.

Up at the flybridge helm, Luke fired up the twin Mercruiser stern drive engines, then he struck the lines and pulled away from the Caddo Bayou Marina, headed on a southerly course. He knew his way without consulting a map. He and Terry had made this trip dozens of times over the years, first with the smaller *Miss Behavin' I,* then after their dot-com windfall, aboard this boat. This was the first time Luke had made it alone.

Well, alone but for a mutt named Knucklehead.

Luke cruised for hours before the lack of sleep caught up with him. After guiding the boat into a protected inlet, he sank the anchors, then sought his bed. The hum of the air conditioner drowned out the songs of Mississippi kites and cardinals drifting on the air, and Luke Callahan drifted off to sleep.

He dreamed of a bikini-clad redhead playing topless beach volleyball and awoke to a bloodcurdling scream.

∾

ALSO BY EMILY MARCH

Lake in the Clouds Women's Fiction Series

THE GETAWAY

BALANCING ACT

The Brazos Bend Contemporary Romance Series

MY BIG OLD TEXAS HEARTACHE

THE LAST BACHELOR IN TEXAS

The Callahan Brothers Trilogy

LUKE—The Callahan Brothers

MATT—The Callahan Brothers

MARK—The Callahan Brothers

A CALLAHAN CAROL

The Eternity Springs Contemporary Romance Series

ANGEL'S REST

HUMMINGBIRD LAKE

HEARTACHE FALLS

MISTLETOE MINE

LOVER'S LEAP

NIGHTINGALE WAY

REFLECTION POINT

MIRACLE ROAD

DREAMWEAVER TRAIL

TEARDROP LANE

HEARTSONG COTTAGE

REUNION PASS

CHRISTMAS IN ETERNITY SPRINGS

A STARDANCE SUMMER

THE FIRST KISS OF SPRING

THE CHRISTMAS WISHING TREE

The Eternity Springs: McBrides of Texas Trilogy

JACKSON

TUCKER

BOONE

Celebrate Eternity Springs Novella Collection

THE CHRISTMAS PAWDCAST novella

BETTER THAN A BOX OF CHOCOLATES novella

THE SUMMER MELT novella

And, SEASON OF SISTERS, a stand alone women's fiction novel.

The Bad Luck Wedding Historical Romance Series

THE BAD LUCK WEDDING DRESS

THE BAD LUCK WEDDING CAKE

Bad Luck Abroad Trilogy

SIMMER ALL NIGHT

SIZZLE ALL DAY

THE BAD LUCK WEDDING NIGHT

Bad Luck Brides Quartet

HER BODYGUARD

HER SCOUNDREL

HER OUTLAW

THE LONER

Stand Alone Historical Romances

THE TEXAN'S BRIDE

CAPTURE THE NIGHT

THE SCOUNDREL'S BRIDE

THE WEDDING RANSOM

THE COWBOY'S RUNAWAY BRIDE

ABOUT THE AUTHOR

Emily March is the *New York Times, Publishers Weekly*, and *USA Today* bestselling author of over forty novels, including the critically acclaimed Eternity Springs series. Publishers Weekly calls March a "master of delightful banter," and her heartwarming, emotionally charged stories have been named to Best of the Year lists by *Publishers Weekly, Library Journal,* and Romance Writers of America.

A graduate of Texas A&M University, Emily is an avid fan of Aggie sports and her recipe for jalapeño relish has made her a tailgating legend.

Emily invites you to register for her newsletter at www.EmilyMarch.com/newsletter